The most comprehensive, illustrated history of the world

WORLD HISTORY

The Middle Ages
1101 – 1460

KING*f*ISHER

Kingfisher an imprint of Larousse plc
Elsley House, 24-30 Great Titchfield Street, London W1P 7AD

This edition published 1997
This edition Copyright © Larousse plc 1997
First published by Kingfisher 1992 as *The Kingfisher Illustrated History of the World*
Copyright © Larousse plc 1992, 1995

British Library Cataloguing-in-Publication Data
A catalogue record for this book is available from the British Library

ISBN 07534 0181 9

Typeset by Tradespools Ltd, Frome, Somerset
Printed in Italy

Contents

The Middle Ages

Travel could be dangerous and difficult in the Middle Ages; nevertheless people journeyed as far afield as China and what were then other unknown places to those living in Europe. Trade was the reason for much of this travel. Silk was carried from China along the Silk Road through Central Asia to the markets of the West. In Africa, caravans trudged across the Sahara, while in the Mediterranean Sea Venetian ships sailed to and fro with their goods. Meanwhile, the merchants of northern Europe grouped themselves together into a trading alliance, the Hanseatic League.

At this time most of Europe was a mass of small kingdoms, principalities, duchies and city-states, which made alliances with each other and then broke apart again. But nationalism, or the sense of belonging to a particular country, was growing, especially in England, France and Scotland.

Empires rose and fell. The Mongol empire, the biggest the world has ever known, came into being and fell apart all within a hundred years. In West Africa, the Mali empire grew powerful, while in eastern Europe the Ottoman empire took the place of the Byzantine empire. Across the Atlantic Ocean, the Incas and the Aztecs were starting to build empires of their own in the Americas.

Many wars were undertaken in the name of religion. Early in the period, Christian knights of Europe set out on crusades to free the Holy Land from the 'infidels', as Christians called the Muslims who controlled Palestine. Later Ottoman Turks captured Constantinople from the people who were 'infidels' to them: the Christians of the Byzantine empire. Meanwhile, the Christian Church was itself divided. At one time there were no fewer than three popes.

By far the most important invention of the Middle Ages came at its close: printing. Suddenly learning came within the reach of everyone who could read.

▼ *Caernarvon Castle in north Wales was built by Edward I of England during his wars with Wales. It was one of the last great castles to be built in Britain.*

The Americas

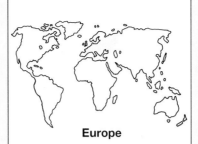

Europe

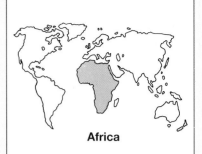

Africa

The Americas	Europe	Africa

1109–1113 War between England and France.
1135 Henry I, King of England, dies.
1143 Portugal becomes independent.

1145–1150 Almohades of North Africa conquer Spain.

1151 End of the Toltec empire.

1152 Eleanor of Aquitaine marries Henry of Anjou.
1170 Thomas à Becket is murdered.

1168 Aztec migration begins.
1191 Second era of Mayan civilization begins.

1190 Henry VI becomes Holy Roman emperor.

1190 Lalibela becomes emperor of Ethiopia.

1200 Hunac Ceel revolts.

1204 France captures Normandy.
1215 Magna Carta agreed.
1223 Mongols invade Russia.

1220 Manco Capac founds the Inca people.

1240 Mongols capture Moscow.

1240 New empire of Mali founded.

1270 Philip III becomes king of France in succession to Louis IX.

1270 Yekuna Amlak becomes emperor of Ethiopia. Louis IX of France dies in Tunis.

1305 Papacy removed to Avignon.

1307 Mansa Musa becomes ruler of Mali. The empire of Benin is established in Nigeria.

1325 The Aztec city of Tenochtitlàn is founded in Mexico.

1326 Queen Isabella leads rebellion against her husband, Edward II, in England.
1337–1453 Hundred Years War between France and England.

1324 Mansa Musa visits Mecca.

1347–1350 Black Death sweeps Europe.
1378–1417 Great Schism.

1438 Inca empire established in Peru.

1460 Wars of the Roses start in England.

1440 Oba Ewuare becomes ruler of Benin.

Near East or Middle East

Asia and the Far East

Australasia and Pacific

1113 Knights of St John founded in Jerusalem.

1143 Manuel Comnenus becomes Byzantine ruler.
1147 Second Crusade begins.

1171 Saladin overthrows Egyptian caliph.
1190 Crusader Emperor Frederick Barbarossa drowned.

1204 Crusaders sack Constantinople.

1261 Michael VIII becomes Byzantine emperor.

1291 End of the Crusades.
1299 Ottoman empire founded in Turkey.
1326 Orkhan I becomes ruler of the Ottoman Turks.

1369 Ottoman Turks attack Bulgaria.

1453 Fall of Constantinople.

1113 Work starts on Angkor Wat.

1190 Temujin begins Mongol conquests.
1192 Minamoto Yoritomo becomes shogun of Japan.
1206 Temujin becomes Genghis Khan.
1218 Mongols conquer Persia.
1219 Hojo clan become shoguns in Japan.
1260 Kublai Khan conquers China.
1271 Marco Polo sets off for China from Venice.

1290 Turkish leader Firuz founds Khalji dynasty in India.
1293 Vijaya founds the Majapahut Empire in Java.
1300s Nō plays are first performed in Japan.

1336 Revolution in Japan.

1368 Ming dynasty begins in China.
1411 Ahmad Shah rules in west India.

A sea slug. Indonesian traders collected them from Australia's north coast.

c. **1200** Tahitians migrate to Hawaii and win control over earlier settlers.

c. **1300** Marco Polo refers to a mythical southern continent.
14th century A second wave of Maoris migrate to New Zealand from the Marquesas, Polynesia.

15th century Indonesian traders regularly visit the northern coast of Australia.

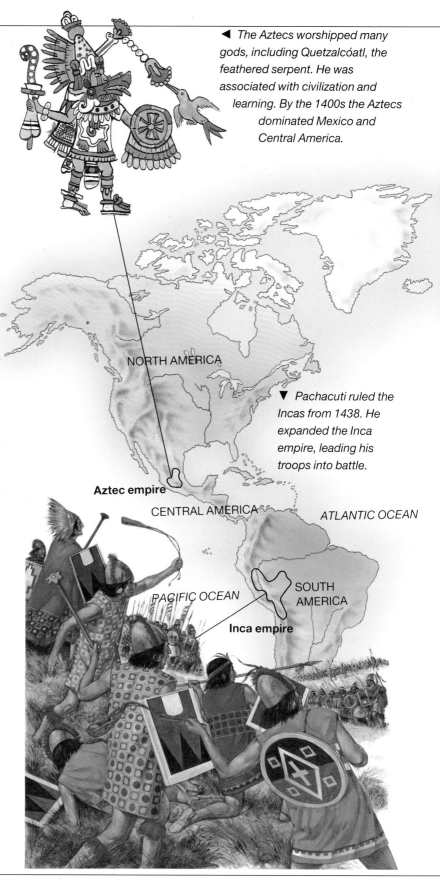

1101–1460

The World

During this period trade increased people's knowledge of many parts of the world, but it also helped to spread the Black Death, a disease carried by fleas which lived on ships' rats. In **Europe**, the Black Death killed a quarter of the population.

Information about **Africa** was spread by Arab traders who sailed down the east coast of the continent. They brought stories of vast inland empires, rich with gold, and centred on large stone cities. In West Africa, the kingdom of Mali flourished.

In the **Far East**, the Khmer empire of Cambodia was at its height. In **Japan**, military rulers called shoguns, supported by samurai warriors were virtual dictators.

The **Mongols** conquered much of Asia and Europe to form the largest empire of all time. Their success was based on brilliant military tactics and superb horsemanship.

In the **Americas**, the Aztecs built their capital city of Tenochtitlán in the centre of a lake in Mexico, while in South America, the Inca empire was expanding by conquering neighbouring tribes.

◄ The Aztecs worshipped many gods, including Quetzalcóatl, the feathered serpent. He was associated with civilization and learning. By the 1400s the Aztecs dominated Mexico and Central America.

NORTH AMERICA

▼ Pachacuti ruled the Incas from 1438. He expanded the Inca empire, leading his troops into battle.

Aztec empire

CENTRAL AMERICA

ATLANTIC OCEAN

PACIFIC OCEAN

SOUTH AMERICA

Inca empire

4

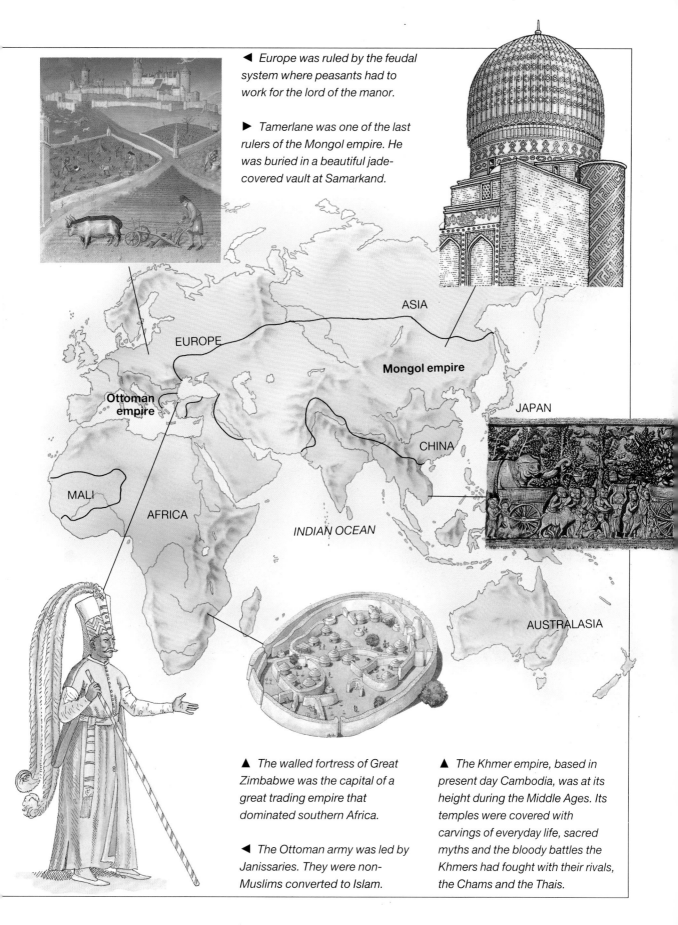

◀ Europe was ruled by the feudal system where peasants had to work for the lord of the manor.

▶ Tamerlane was one of the last rulers of the Mongol empire. He was buried in a beautiful jade-covered vault at Samarkand.

ASIA

EUROPE

Mongol empire

JAPAN

Ottoman empire

CHINA

MALI

AFRICA

INDIAN OCEAN

AUSTRALASIA

▲ The walled fortress of Great Zimbabwe was the capital of a great trading empire that dominated southern Africa.

◀ The Ottoman army was led by Janissaries. They were non-Muslims converted to Islam.

▲ The Khmer empire, based in present day Cambodia, was at its height during the Middle Ages. Its temples were covered with carvings of everyday life, sacred myths and the bloody battles the Khmers had fought with their rivals, the Chams and the Thais.

1104 Palestine: Crusaders capture the Muslim city of Acre.

1106 Germany: Henry V becomes Holy Roman emperor (to 1125). England: Henry I defeats his brother Robert, Duke of Normandy, at battle of Tinchebrai: Robert remains captive for life.

1107 Scotland: Alexander I is king (to 1124).

1108 France: Louis VI is king (to 1137).

1109 War breaks out between England and France (until 1113).

1111 Holy Roman emperor Henry V forces Pope Paschal II to acknowledge his power.

Weapons like these axes and sword were commonly used in battle by knights during the Crusades.

1113 Palestine: Knights of St John founded. Cambodia: Work starts on Angkor Wat.

1114 England: Matilda (Maud), daughter of King Henry I, marries Holy Roman emperor Henry V.

1115 France: St Bernard founds the Abbey of Clairvaux, and becomes its first abbot. Hungary: Stephen II is king (to 1131).

1118 Byzantine empire: John II Comnenus becomes emperor (to 1143); he revives Byzantine power.

1119 Palestine: Hugues de Payens founds the Order of Knights Templar.

c. 1120 China: Playing cards are invented.

1120 England: Prince William, heir to Henry I, drowns when the *White Ship* is lost in the English Channel.

The Crusades

To Christians everywhere, Palestine, where Jesus Christ lived and died, was the Holy Land. Pilgrims travelled there from all over Europe from the 2nd century onward. Even after the Muslim Arabs conquered Palestine, pilgrims were free to come and go as they wished. But when the Seljuk Turks, who were also Muslims, invaded the land from central Asia, they persecuted the Christians.

Pope Urban II called on Christian leaders to free the Holy Land from the infidels, as Christians called the Muslims. Because the knights who went to Palestine wore a cross, the expeditions are known as the Crusades, from the Spanish word *cruzada* which means 'marked with the Cross'.

The first Crusaders were a disorganized band, led by two well-meaning men named Peter the Hermit and Walter the Penniless. They never reached Palestine. Later a well-disciplined army recaptured Jerusalem and set up four Christian kingdoms in Palestine. At first the Saracens, as the Crusaders called the Seljuk Turks, left the kingdoms alone.

▼ *Armies from France and Italy journeyed across Europe to the Holy Land. They travelled by way of Constantinople, capital of the Byzantine empire.*

▲ *A 14th century picture of Crusaders boarding ship and loading supplies at a French Mediterranean port.*

But eight more Crusades followed, and by the end of the 13th century the Christians had been thrown out.

Many of the Crusaders were more interested in personal gain than religion, and they quarrelled among themselves. By the 14th Century, Europe had lost interest in the Crusades. Although there were several more attempts to organize Crusades, they all failed.

▼ *Richard I of England led an army to Jerusalem, but was unable to recapture it from the Saracens.*

CHILDREN'S CRUSADE

In 1212 several thousand boys and girls decided to march and save the Holy Land. Some were sold into slavery on the way, others were turned back. From this may have come the legend of the Pied Piper of Hamelin, who lured a band of children away.

▼ *The crossed legs of this effigy on the tomb of a Norman knight show he had been on a crusade.*

Knighthood

Warfare was the most important occupation for a young man of good family at the time of the Crusades. But knighthood was not just about fighting. A knight was expected to be just and honourable as well as brave, to help the weak and protect the poor. These qualities formed the ideal known as chivalry, though many knights did not live up to these high standards.

Boys began their training at about the age of seven, as pages in the household of a knight or nobleman. At the age of 14 or 15 a page was promoted to squire, the personal attendant of a knight. A squire served at table, helped his master to put on his armour, and accompanied him into battle. He spent many hours practising riding and the use of the sword and lance. After a few years he too was made a knight, especially if he had fought well in battle.

► Two orders of knights active during the Crusades were the Knights Templar (left) and the Knights of St John (right), also known as Hospitallers because they set up a hospital for pilgrims in Jerusalem. Their long robes, or surcoats, kept the hot sun off their armour.

◄ Two knights jousting (fighting) in a tournament. They used blunt swords and lances, but even so knights were often killed or maimed. Tournaments showed the skills and bravery of knighthood. They became very organized in the 15th century with rules on issuing a challenge, fighting and scoring points. Mock sieges and assaults on castles were also staged.

▲ *The troubadour tradition of poetry and music first started in the 11th century in southern France. These minstrels sang songs of love, chivalry and religion.*

Knights continued to practise their skills, often in mock battles called tournaments. During these, most knights carried a token from a lady, such as a scarf or glove, to show they were fighting on her behalf. Two kings, Richard I of England and Louis IX of France, were famous for their support of the romantic ideals of chivalry.

▼ *A squire kneels to help his master arm for battle. Plate armour of steel was introduced in the 14th century. Before that knights wore chain mail.*

1122 The Concordat of Worms, a conference of German princes, ends the dispute between the pope and the Holy Roman emperor over appointing bishops.

1123 Persia: Death of poet Omar Khayyam.

1124 Scotland: David I, younger brother of Alexander I, becomes king (to 1153).

1125 Holy Roman Empire: Lothair of Saxony is elected emperor (to 1137).

1126 Spain: Alfonso VII, King of Castile (to 1157). China: The Song dynasty loses control of north China.

1129 France: Matilda, widow of Henry V, marries Geoffrey of Anjou.

c. 1135 England: Geoffrey of Monmouth writes *History of the Kings of Britain* which includes stories about King Arthur.

The highest duty of a chivalrous knight was to protect vulnerable people.

1135 England: Stephen of Blois seizes the crown on the death of his uncle, Henry I; a rival claim by Matilda causes civil war.

1137 France: Louis VII becomes king (to 1180).

1138 Scotland: David I is defeated at the battle of the Standard while fighting on behalf of Matilda. France: Louis VII marries Eleanor of Aquitaine. Holy Roman Empire: Conrad III becomes emperor (to 1152).

1139 England: Matilda arrives from France.

Arts and Crafts

In Europe, the arts of stained glass and tapestry flourished. They were used to show illustrated versions of Bible stories, so that people who could not read might learn from them instead.

Later artists began to paint pictures as though they were 'windows on the world'. The colours they used were brighter and they painted on wood, walls and canvas.

Many plays were on religious subjects. These included Mystery Plays which were based on the Bible. Poems were about popular heroes such as Charlemagne and King Arthur. Poets began to write in the national languages instead of Latin.

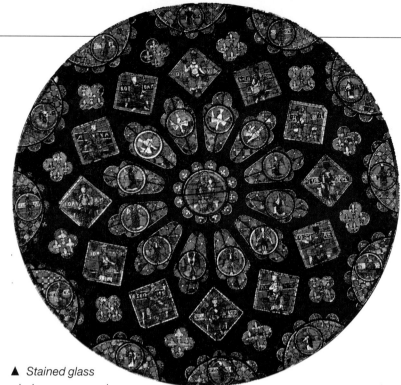

▲ Stained glass windows were made from pieces of coloured glass, joined together with strips of lead. This is the Rose of France window at Chartres Cathedral.

▼ There were no theatres in Europe in the Middle Ages. Plays were performed in the street, with a cart for the stage.

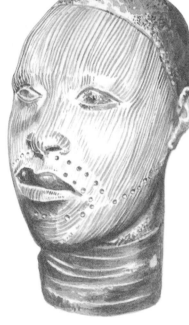

▲ The people of the African kingdom of Benin were skilled workers in iron, bronze and ivory. They were famous for their sculptures of human heads. Some were made from clay and hardened into pottery, but the best ones were cast in bronze.

▲ Wooden furniture and wall panels were often carved or painted with scenes from stories. This scene is from The Pardoner's Tale by Chaucer. It shows Death teaching a lesson to three men.

▶ These two Aztec women are making cloth. One is spinning raw cotton into yarn for the other to weave on a belt-loom. It is given this name because one end is attached to the woman's belt.

◀ During the Ming dynasty (1368–1644) the Chinese started to make blue-and-white pottery in imperial factories. Later, much of it was exported to Europe.

▼ Jan van Eyck painted The Arnolfini Wedding in 1434. By then portraits were more realistic and rich people commissioned them for their homes.

WHEN IT HAPPENED

1307 Dante Alighieri in Florence, Italy, writes *The Divine Comedy*.

1348 Giovanni Boccaccio starts to write *The Decameron*, a book of stories told by people fleeing from the plague.

1360 William Langland, the English poet, writes *The Vision of Piers Plowman*.

1368 The Persian poet Há fiz, publishes the love poem *The Diwan*.

1388 The English poet, Geoffrey Chaucer, writes *The Canterbury Tales*.

1415 Following Roman models, Donatello sculpts unusually realistic statues of St Mark and St George in Italy.

1140 Venice: The power of the doge (Venetian ruler) is transferred to a Great Council.

1141 England: Matilda captures Stephen at the battle of Lincoln. Her reign is disastrous, and Stephen is restored.

1143 Alfonso Henriques, Count of Portugal, makes Portugal independent of Spain and becomes king (to 1185). Byzantine empire: Manuel Comnenus rules (to 1180).

1145 Spain: Almohades, North African Berber dynasty, begin the conquest of Moorish Spain (to 1150).

1147 England: Matilda leaves for France. Palestine: The Second Crusade begins (ends 1149). Crusaders fail to capture Damascus.

***c.* 1150** First paper made in Europe.

1150 France: Founding of Paris University. Cambodia: Temple at Angkor Wat completed by Suryavaraman II.

1151 France: Geoffrey of Anjou dies. Mexico: Toltec empire comes to an end.

The seal of Paris University, first used in 1215. In 1258 Robert de Sorbon founded a religious college at Paris University, now called the Sorbonne.

1152 France: Marriage of Louis VII and Eleanor of Aquitaine is annulled. Eleanor marries Henry of Anjou, adding Aquitaine to the regions of Anjou and Normandy that Henry already rules. Holy Roman Empire: Frederick I Barbarossa becomes emperor (to 1190).

1153 England: Henry of Anjou, son of Matilda, invades England and forces Stephen to make him heir to the throne. Scotland: Malcolm IV, 'The Maiden', grandson of David I, rules (to 1165).

1154 England: Henry of Anjou becomes King Henry II (to 1189); he also rules more than half of France. Papacy: Nicholas Breakspear becomes Adrian IV (to 1159), the only English pope.

Henry of Anjou

The way to the throne was not an easy one for Henry II of England. His mother, Matilda, was the daughter of Henry I, who wanted her to be the next ruler of England. But the throne was seized by her cousin Stephen and civil war broke out. Matilda was the widow of the Holy Roman emperor, Henry V. She next married Count Geoffrey of Anjou, in France. Their son, Henry, forced Stephen to make him his heir.

By the time Henry II became king of England at the age of 21, he had inherited Anjou, Maine, Touraine and Normandy in France from his parents. He gained Aquitaine when he married its beautiful duchess, Eleanor.

Henry chose capable people for his ministers, among them Thomas à Becket, a priest who became chancellor. As the king's chief minister, Becket led a life of pomp and power. But when Henry made

▼ *Henry II ruled over a greater area of France than the French king Louis VII, though Louis looked after Henry's French lands.*

ELEANOR

Eleanor of Aquitaine (c. 1122–1204) married Louis VII of France in 1138. The marriage was annulled and in 1152 she married Henry of Anjou becoming queen of England in 1154.

PLANTAGENET

Henry II's father, Geoffrey of Anjou, wore a sprig of broom (called *planta genista* in Latin) in his cap. Because of this people called him Plantagenet and the name passed to his descendants.

him archbishop of Canterbury, Becket changed his ways. He led a frugal life and began to assert the rights of the Church. After years of quarrels, Henry exclaimed crossly, 'Who will rid me of this turbulent priest?' Four knights took him at his word and killed Becket. Henry did penance for this crime, but it made little difference to him. He forced the king of the Scots to do homage to him, invaded Ireland and subdued the Welsh.

▲ Eleanor of Aquitaine's tomb in the abbey church at Frontrevault, in western France, lies next to one of her sons, Richard I. Her husband Henry II lies nearby.

▼ The Archbishop of Canterbury, Thomas à Becket, was brutally murdered by four of King Henry II's knights on the altar steps of Canterbury Cathedral.

THOMAS A BECKET

Becket (1118–1170) became archbishop of Canterbury in 1162. He opposed the king and fled to France. On his return in 1170 he was murdered. He was made a saint in 1173.

Ireland

Ireland in the early 12th century was made up of more than 100 small kingdoms that often fought each other. Even so, the Irish were united because they all spoke the same language, Irish-Gaelic, and belonged to the Celtic Christian Church. Most of them were Celts, but some descendants of the Vikings lived in the east.

The five largest kingdoms were Ulster, Leinster, Munster, Connaught and Meath. One of their kings usually held the title of *Ard Ri* (high king). The last really strong high king was Turlough O'Connor, King of Connaught. After he died, his son Rory made himself high king. But the King of Leinster, Dermot MacMurrough, also wanted the title.

Dermot asked for help from the Normans who ruled England. Eventually Richard de Clare, Earl of Pembroke, known as 'Strongbow', agreed to back him in return for marrying Dermot's daughter, Aoife, and inheriting Leinster. As King of Leinster, Strongbow, and other Normans, seized Irish lands for themselves. This alarmed the king of England, Henry II, who proclaimed himself overlord of Ireland.

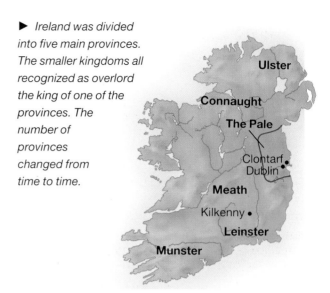

► *Ireland was divided into five main provinces. The smaller kingdoms all recognized as overlord the king of one of the provinces. The number of provinces changed from time to time.*

HIGH KINGS OF IRELAND

The first high king of Ireland was Cormac mac Airt of Tara in the 3rd century. The greatest of them was Brian Boru, King of Munster, who died after defeating Viking invaders at the battle of Clontarf in 1014. For the next 100 years the kingdoms fought bitterly amongst themselves until Turlough O'Conner, King of Connaught, became the most powerful king in Ireland. He built fortresses and weakened his rivals by dividing their kingdoms.

▼ *On the Rock of Cashel stand the ruins of St Patrick's Cathedral. Given to the Church in 1101, the cross (far left) is where the kings of Munster were crowned.*

BREHON LAWS

Each Irish kingdom had its own judge, called a brehon. Over hundreds of years, the brehons built up a system of laws called the Brehon Laws. These laws covered property, trade and contracts. They allowed a woman to manage her own property, but never that which belonged to her husband.

STRONGBOW

Richard de Clare, known as Strongbow, (c. 1130–1176) became earl of Pembroke in 1148. In 1170 he invaded Ireland and afterwards was made king of Leinster in 1171.

Like the Vikings before them, many Normans adopted the customs of the Irish. In 1366, Edward III's son, Lionel, who was in charge of Ireland, ordered the Normans to stop speaking Irish and forbade them to marry Irish women. But the Irish gradually reclaimed their lands and by the late 15th century English rule was confined to a small area around Dublin called 'the Pale'.

▼ The marriage of the tough Norman warrior Strongbow to Aoife, daughter of the King of Leinster, paved the way for the Normans to take over Irish lands.

1155 England: Henry II makes Thomas à Becket Chancellor. Pope Adrian IV grants Henry II the right to rule Ireland.

1156 Japan: Civil wars start between rival clans (to 1185).

1158 Spain: Alfonso VIII becomes king of Castile (to 1214).

1159 England: Henry II demands scutage (payment in cash) instead of military service. Papacy: Alexander III becomes pope (to 1181).

1161 China: Explosives are used at the battle of Ts'ai-shih.

1162 England: Becket appointed archbishop of Canterbury; at once he quarrels with Henry II over the Church's rights.

1164 England: Becket flees to France.

1168 Mexico: Aztecs begin to migrate.

The knight from the Canterbury Tales, *written in 1388 by Geoffrey Chaucer.*

1169 Egypt: Saladin (Salah al-Din), becomes vizier (to 1193) and sultan from 1174.

1170 England: Becket is apparently reconciled with King Henry II and returns to Canterbury, but is murdered soon afterward. Oxford University is founded. Ireland: Normans from England invade under the command of Strongbow.

1171 England: Henry II breaks the power of Strongbow and annexes Ireland.

1173 England: Henry's sons, Henry, Richard, and Geoffrey, rebel supported by their mother, Eleanor of Aquitaine. Thomas à Becket is declared a saint.

1174 Palestine: Saladin conquers Syria.

Buildings

Most people in Europe built their houses with wood because it was cheap and plentiful. Unfortunately, it caught fire easily. This was a big danger in towns where houses were close together and a fire could spread quickly. In time, wood rotted so important buildings were built with stone. Special stone was sometimes brought long distances to build cathedrals and churches.

Cathedrals were built in a new style called Gothic which replaced the Romanesque style. This change meant that instead of rounded arches and sturdy pillars, churches had pointed arches and slender pillars. They also had larger windows.

Castles were also built with stone, and towns without a castle to protect them were usually surrounded by a high stone wall.

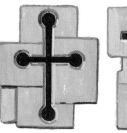

▲ Most castle walls had slots called loopholes. They were narrow on the outside and wide on the inside. This let the defenders shoot arrows out, but attackers could not shoot arrows in. Some sloped at the bottom so that the archer could fire downwards.

▼ A baron's castle was his home. It was also the place from which he looked after his estates and defended the surrounding countryside. Many castles were built on hills or beside rivers to make it more difficult for any enemies to get close.

Carpenter

Mixing mortar

Blacksmith

◀ Hundreds of workmen were needed to build a cathedral, an abbey or a castle. Carpenters cut the wood to the right length and shape. They also made the scaffolding for the builders to climb on. Other men burned lime and mixed it with sand and water. This made the mortar which was used to stick the stones together. Meanwhile the blacksmith made nails, and made and mended tools.

▶ Gothic style churches were taller and lighter than earlier ones. They took many years to build. Note the pointed arches.

▲ Two important workers were the stone cutter (above) and the mason (below). The cutter shaped stones and numbered them so that the mason knew where they went.

WHEN IT HAPPENED

1163 Work starts on the Gothic cathedral of Notre Dame in Paris, France.
1200 Early English Gothic style starts.
1300 Decorated phase of English Gothic architecture starts.
1370 Perpendicular phase of English Gothic architecture starts (ends about 1540).
1420 Filippo Brunelleschi starts work on Florence Cathedral, Italy.

▶ Stone carvers left their own special marks to identify their work. Some of them also carved the faces of the people they knew on the gargoyles and other decorations around the churches they built.

1177 Palestine: Baldwin IV of Jerusalem defeats Saladin at Montgisard.
1179 Palestine: Saladin besieges Tyre. Truce agreed between Baldwin IV and Saladin. Mongolia: Temujin becomes leader.
1181 Cambodia: Jayarvarman VII is made king (to 1220).
1183 Byzantine empire: Reformer Andronicus I becomes emperor.
1185 Portugal: Sancho I is king (to 1211). Byzantine empire: Andronicus I is executed, a period of corruption follows. Isaac II becomes emperor (to 1195). Japan: Kamakura period (to 1333).
1187 Palestine: Saladin captures Jerusalem.

Saladin, Sultan of Egypt and Syria and great Muslim warrior, taken from a Persian portrait.

1189 England: Richard I becomes king of England (to 1199). Palestine: Third Crusade starts (to 1192). North America: The Vikings visit for the last time.
1190 Holy Roman Empire: Frederick Barbarossa is drowned on his way to Palestine. Henry VI becomes Holy Roman emperor (to 1197). Ethiopia: Lalibela is made emperor (to 1225). Mongolia: Temujin begins conquests.
1191 Palestine: Richard I of England conquers Cyprus and captures Acre in Third Crusade. North America: Second era of Mayan civilization begins.
1192 Palestine: Richard I of England captures Jaffa, makes peace with Saladin but on the way home he is captured by his enemy, Duke Leopold of Austria. Japan: Minamoto Yoritomo becomes shogun.

Shoguns and Samurai

The Fujiwara family had held power in Japan from the 9th century. However, the influence of the Fujiwara family broke down when they ran out of daughters, the traditional brides of the emperor. For a time retired emperors ruled. Then the Taira clan took over briefly until a rival clan, the Minamoto, whom the Taira had defeated, rallied under Minamoto Yoritomo and seized power. Yoritomo assumed the title of *sei-i dai-shogun* which means 'barbarian conquering great general'. His appointment in 1192 was without limit to his authority and from then on shoguns ruled Japan as hereditary military dictators until 1868. Minamoto set up his military government in Kamakura, after which his shogunate is named. When Minamoto died in 1199 the Hojo family, a branch of the Taira

▼ The ruthless general Minamoto Yoritomo lived from 1147 to 1199. A brilliant organizer, he let others take command in battles and had his rivals murdered.

clan, took control of Japan.

The shoguns were members of a warrior class, called *samurai*. Samurai were prepared to fight to the death for their *daimyos* (overlords), to whom they swore undying loyalty. Like the medieval knights in Europe, samurai believed in the values of truth and honour.

In battle a samurai fought hand to hand, on foot or on horseback. Before combat he shouted his name and those of his ancestors, and boasted of his own heroic deeds. If he was dishonoured he was expected to commit suicide. The samurai also lost their status in 1868.

▲ *A samurai took a long time to arm himself for battle. He always took a bath first so that he would be clean and sweet-smelling if he were killed.*

▼ *A samurai's chief weapons were a bow of boxwood or bamboo and a single edged sword. Samurai were trained from childhood and followed a strict code called* Bushido *(warrior's way). Battles were almost ceremonial, with a series of individual duels accompanied by chants, flag signals, drums and gongs.*

ARMS AND ARMOUR

A samurai wore elaborate armour, made of enamelled iron plates sewn on to fabric. He carried a sword and a dagger and often a fan reinforced with iron plates, which was used as a shield. His mask was designed to make him look fierce.

European Trade

The early Middle Ages were a period of great prosperity for Europe. The population was growing which meant more land needed to be cultivated to grow food. Eventually this led to an agricultural surplus which could be traded. Towns grew up as trade centres and markets. Some, such as the French town of Troyes, were the site of regular trade fairs. Others, such as Paris or London, stood on important road and river links. Many were sea ports as it was often easiest to travel by water.

Italy was one of the main trade centres. The Crusades weakened Islam's control of the Mediterranean Sea and through Venice, Genoa and other ports came spices, silks and other riches of the East. Goods from Asia travelled either overland along the Silk Road or by ship from India to the Red Sea and overland to the Mediterranean. They were exchanged for cloth, furs, hides, iron, linen, timber and slaves.

Most of Europe's money was silver, but the Asian countries traded in gold. This

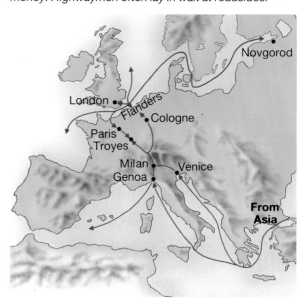

▲ The perils of medieval travel are shown by this drawing of a highwayman robbing a traveller of his money. Highwaymen often lay in wait at roadsides.

▼ Market day in a medieval town. Markets were usually held once a week. Livestock, food, metal, leather and woodwork were all sold.

▲ Trade routes in the 12th century. Italian merchants attended fairs such as Troyes to buy Flemish cloth and sell Asian goods.

caused problems so Italian merchants invented banking with bills of exchange which could be used instead of cash.

In northern Europe trade was centred on the Rhineland in Germany, with the city of Cologne at the height of its prosperity. The Low Countries (now Belgium and the Netherlands) imported raw materials such as copper and wool and sold manufactured (finished) goods. During this time England began to sell most of its surplus wool to Flanders (now part of Belgium) where it was made into richly coloured cloth.

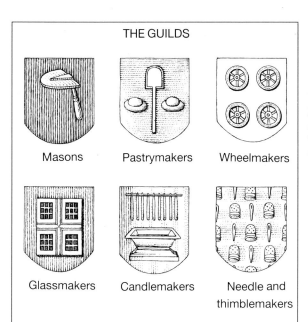

THE GUILDS

Masons Pastrymakers Wheelmakers

Glassmakers Candlemakers Needle and thimblemakers

Guilds had existed on a family basis since Anglo-Saxon times but were eventually formed for all merchants and craftsmen. They regulated trade and set standards. Apprentices could serve for up to 12 years before becoming a master. To qualify, an apprentice submitted a piece of work, called a masterpiece. Shown are some emblems of guilds.

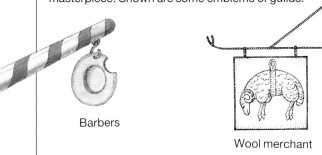

Barbers

Wool merchant

1193 Austria: Leopold hands Richard I of England over to Holy Roman Emperor Henry VI, who demands a ransom. Palestine: Saladin dies and Al-Aziz Imad al-Din succeeds him (to 1198). India: Muslims capture Bihar and Bengal under Muhammad of Ghur (Mu'izz-ud-din).

1194 Holy Roman Empire: Henry VI conquers Sicily. Richard I is ransomed and returns to England. According to legend the place where Richard I is imprisoned was found by his troubadour, Blondel, who had accompanied him on the Crusades.

1195 Spain: Pedro II becomes king of Aragon (to 1213). Byzantine empire: Alexius III is made emperor (to 1203).

A money balance was used by both bankers and merchants to weigh solid silver coins to find out their value.

1197 Holy Roman Empire: Henry VI dies and civil war breaks out. Bohemia: Ottakar I becomes king (to 1230).

1198 Holy Roman Empire: Otto IV becomes emperor (to 1212). Papacy: Innocent III is made pope (to 1216).

1199 England: Henry II's youngest son, John, becomes king (to 1216).

c. 1200 Europe: Compass first used. Trade undergoes great expansion owing to the growing number of towns that require goods of all types. Polynesia: People from the island of Tahiti arrive in Hawaii and win control over the earlier settlers.

1200 North America: Hunac Ceel revolts against the Mayas of Chichén Itzá and sets up a new capital at Mayapan.

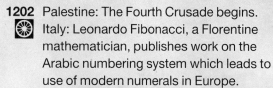

1202 Palestine: The Fourth Crusade begins.
 Italy: Leonardo Fibonacci, a Florentine mathematician, publishes work on the Arabic numbering system which leads to use of modern numerals in Europe.

1203 England: John orders his nephew Arthur, Duke of Brittany, the true heir to the throne, to be murdered.

1204 France: Philip II captures Normandy and Touraine from England. Fourth Crusade: Crusaders, unable to pay Venice for transport, agree to loot Constantinople on Venice's behalf.

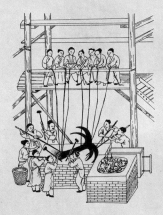

By the 14th century skilled, Chinese iron workers knew how to forge metal objects such as this huge ship's anchor.

1206 Mongolia: Temujin is proclaimed Genghis Khan, 'Emperor of All Men'.

1207 England: Pope Innocent III appoints Stephen Langton archbishop of Canterbury but King John does not allow him to take office.

1209 England: Innocent III excommunicates John for attacks on Church property; Cambridge University is founded.

1210 Holy Roman Empire: Innocent III excommunicates Emperor Otto IV. Italy: Francis of Assisi founds the Franciscan Order. Mongolia: Genghis Khan begins the invasion of China.

1211 Portugal: Alfonso II is king (to 1223).

1212 Holy Roman Empire: Frederick II is made emperor (to 1250). Children's Crusade: thousands of children from France and Germany set off for Palestine.

The Rise of Venice

When the Roman empire fell in the 5th century, a group of Roman citizens from the northern end of the Adriatic Sea fled to the safety of lagoons further down the coast. They settled on some muddy islands and so began one of the greatest Italian cities: Venice.

The people built on stilts. There was no land to farm, so the early Venetians turned to the sea to fish. Their small boats then ventured further afield to trade. The Venetians constructed more permanent homes, on piles driven into the mud, and channelled the sea so that it flowed in canals between the islands.

By 1100 Venice was a wealthy place. Protected by the sea, it did not have to spend time and money building elaborate fortifications. Its rich traders lived in sumptuous palaces and expanded their influence in the Near East by taking an active part in the Crusades. After fighting off its great trading rival Genoa, Venetian ships handled most of the trade between northern Europe and the Far East. Venice reached the height of its power during the 15th century with an empire which included many Greek islands, Cyprus, the Dalmatian coast (now in

▲ *The Lion of St Mark has been Venice's emblem for centuries. The lion is often shown straddling the land and sea symbolizing Venice's dominance of both.*

▶ *Venice in the Middle Ages was well placed both for safety and for trade. It was Europe's greatest port for hundreds of years, and the main trading link between west and east.*

▼ *Four bronze horses, dating from the 4th century BC, were seized by the Venetians at the sack of Constantinople in 1204 during the Fourth Crusade. The Crusades enabled Venice to grow even richer.*

GOODS TRADED

Twice a year a fleet of ships sailed from Venice to the Levant in the eastern Mediterranean, guarded by war galleys. It carried amber, metals including gold and silverware, linen, timber and woollen cloth. The fleet returned with cotton, silk and porcelain from China, spices from Zanzibar and the East Indies, gems and ivory from Burma (Myanmar) and India, and dyewood from which dyes and pigments were extracted. Venice itself was famous for its lace and glassware and for a long time the only mirrors made were made in Venice.

Croatia) and part of north-eastern Italy.
Like other places in medieval Italy, Venice was a city-state, largely independent. Its rulers were called *doges*, from the Latin word *dux* which means a leader. Doges were elected for life and came from among the most powerful and wealthy families in Venice. They had almost absolute power over government, the army and church. But after 1140 they lost most of their powers which were transferred to a Great Council.

Communications

The biggest revolution in communications in Europe came in the middle of the 15th century when Johannes Gutenberg began to print books using movable metal type. Although there had been some wood block printing in Europe before this time, it took a long time to cut each block and it could only be used for one page in one book. With movable type, many copies of one page could be printed, then the type could be rearranged and used for another page. This was far quicker than copying out books by hand, and so more books became available for those who could read.

For most people, however, the only form of communication was by word of mouth. Traders often spread news as they went on their travels, and villagers brought it back from market. This meant that news was months out of date, and often wrong.

The reason why news travelled slowly was that people themselves travelled slowly. On land the top speed was still that of the fastest horse, while at sea ships depended on the wind to provide them with power.

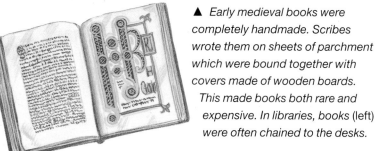

▲ Early medieval books were completely handmade. Scribes wrote them on sheets of parchment which were bound together with covers made of wooden boards. This made books both rare and expensive. In libraries, books (left) were often chained to the desks.

▲ Once people started printing with movable type, books could be produced more quickly and more efficiently. Although this made books cheaper, only the rich could afford them or knew how to read.

◄ *Travellers in Asia and the Middle East often had to cross vast areas of desert with no towns or villages to stay in or buy food. To solve the problem, caravanserais were built along the main routes. They provided food and rooms for the travellers, and fodder, water and shelter for their horses and camels. The caravanserais also gave travellers the chance to meet up and pass on information about the road ahead.*

▼ *Mediterranean sailors, copying Arab boats, started to use a triangular or lateen sail, which could be swung into the wind.*

WHEN IT HAPPENED

1271 Marco Polo sets out from Venice to visit China. He later writes about his travels.

1397 The oldest surviving books printed with movable type are produced in Korea.

1434 Portuguese sailors round Cape Bojador off the coast of West Africa.

1440 Gutenberg starts using movable type in Germany.

▼ *In Europe posting stations were built along main roads. They served refreshments to travellers, who could also change their horses or have them reshod.*

Charter and Parliament

King John of England, the youngest son of Henry II, was given to violent bursts of temper. Not surprisingly, he soon annoyed his barons in English-ruled Anjou and Poitiers, and he lost those lands. In England, he taxed his barons heavily and ignored their rights until they rebelled. The barons demanded that John should confirm their ancient rights. They met him in a meadow called Runnymede, beside the River Thames. There they forced the king to put his seal to the Magna Carta, which means 'great charter'.

No sooner had John agreed to the Charter than he went back on his word. But he died the following year, leaving the throne to his nine-year-old son, who

▲ *The Great Seal of King John affixed to the bottom of the Magna Carta. John's seal showed his agreement and so turned the Charter into the law of the land.*

▼ *A 19th century artist's impression of King John signing the Magna Carta. In fact he did not actually sign it, and possibly could not even write.*

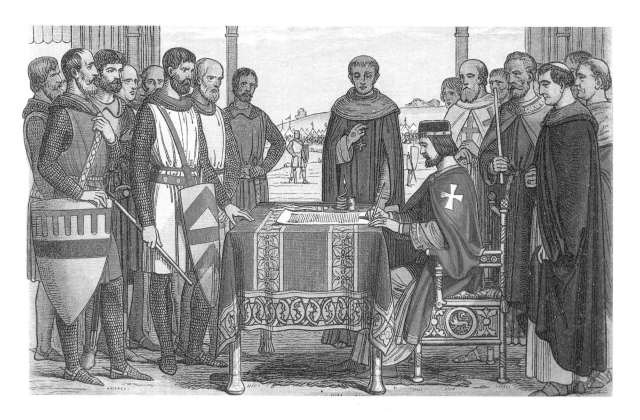

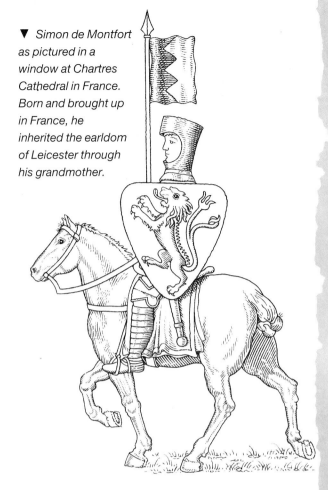

▼ *Simon de Montfort as pictured in a window at Chartres Cathedral in France. Born and brought up in France, he inherited the earldom of Leicester through his grandmother.*

1213 England: Pope Innocent III declares John deposed. John hurriedly makes peace with him. John surrenders the kingdom to the pope and becomes his vassal. Spain: James I, the Conqueror, becomes king of Aragon (to 1276).
1215 England: The barons force John to agree to a statement of their rights in the Magna Carta. France: St Dominic founds the Dominican Order of friars at Toulouse.
1216 England: Henry III, aged nine, becomes king (to 1272). Papacy: Honorius III is made pope (to 1227).
1217 Fifth Crusade (to 1222); the venture fails to capture Egypt.
1218 Genghis Khan conquers Persia.
1219 Mongols conquer Bokhara. Japan: Hojo clan rules (to 1333), after they overthrow the Minamoto family.
1220 According to tradition, Manco Capac founds the Inca civilization in Peru.
1223 France: Louis VIII becomes king (to 1226). Russia: Mongols invade.
1225 England: A revised version of the Magna Carta is issued.

Images of monkeys were often used to mock people who took things too seriously. Rabbits, geese and foxes were also used to make fun.

1226 France: Louis IX, aged 12, becomes king of France (to 1270). His mother, Blanche of Castile, becomes regent and dominates European politics for the next quarter of a century.
1227 England: Henry III, now aged 20, begins to rule. Papacy: Gregory IX becomes pope (to 1241). Mongolia: Genghis Khan dies.

became Henry III. The barons had the Charter reissued, and in 1225 it became the law of England. The Charter stated that the king could continue to rule, but must keep to the laws of the land and could be compelled to do so.

Henry III was incompetent and spent large sums of money. Again the barons got together, led by Simon de Montfort. They forced Henry to agree to rule with the help of a council of barons if they paid off his debts. Like his father, Henry III went back on the deal, but de Montfort defeated him in battle at Lewes and ruled the country in Henry's name. In 1265, de Montfort called a Parliament (governing body) at which he asked for two knights from every shire and two burgesses from every town to attend. This was the first time commoners had attended; up to then parliaments had consisted only of barons and bishops.

1228 Sixth Crusade (to 1229): Led by Holy Roman Emperor Frederick II, Crusaders recapture Jerusalem.

1229 Mongolia: Ogodai, son of Genghis, is elected khan (to 1241).

1232 The earliest known rockets are used in a war between Mongols and Chinese.

1233 England: Coal is first mined in Newcastle-upon-Tyne.

1234 China: Mongols annex the Chin empire of north China.

1235 Mali: Sundiata Keita is king (to 1255).

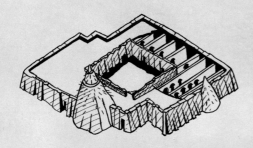

The great mosque at Timbuktu was designed by As-Saheli, an Egyptian.

1236 Russia: Alexander Nevski is made prince of Novgorod (to 1263).

1238 Spain: First European paper mills appear at Sativa.

1240 Russia: Alexander Nevski of Novgorod defeats the Swedes at the battle of Neva. Mongols capture Moscow and destroy Kiev. West Africa: Old empire of Ghana is incorporated in the new kingdom of Mali.

1241 Mongols invade Hungary and cross the River Danube into Austria; they are forced to withdraw from Europe following the death of their leader Ogodai Khan.

1242 Russia: Batu, grandson of Genghis Khan, establishes Mongol khanate of Kipchak, known as the Golden Horde, on the lower Volga River.

1243 Papacy: Innocent IV becomes pope (to 1254). Palestine: Egyptians capture Jerusalem from the Christians.

1245 Holy Roman Empire: Pope Innocent IV calls the Synod of Lyon, which declares Emperor Frederick II deposed.

Mali and Ethiopia

In 1240 Sundiata Keita, ruler of the small West African kingdom of Kangaba, brought to an end the empire of Ghana and established a new empire, Mali. Under his rule the empire soon became rich and powerful, reaching its peak under Sundiata's grandson Mansa Musa in the early 14th century.

The empire covered a large part of what is now Gambia, Senegal, Guinea and Mali. Its merchants traded gold, kola nuts and slaves for cloth, copper, dates, figs, metal goods and salt. All these travelled by caravans of camels across the Sahara from northern Africa.

Timbuktu, on the River Niger and now in modern Mali, became the capital and chief trading centre. When Mansa Musa converted the empire to Islam, Timbuktu became a centre of Muslim scholarship

▼ *Mansa Musa as shown in the Catalan Atlas of 1375. He made a famous pilgrimage to Mecca, accompanied by 500 slaves and many camels carrying gold.*

CHURCHES

Ethiopia was the only Christian country in Africa. During the 13th century, the emperors of Ethiopia had 11 Christian churches carved out of solid rock. One of the most remarkable was the Church of St George at Lalibela, in the mountains north of Addis Ababa. To build the church, workers had to cut a hole 12 metres deep in the rock, leaving a cross-shaped block standing in the middle. They then hollowed out the middle of this block to form the interior of the church.

FALASHA JEWS

Ethiopia has about 20,000 people, called Falashas, who follow the Jewish faith. Because they have no ancient Jewish traditions, it is thought they were converted at the beginning of the Christian era. The Falashas, like the former emperors of Ethiopia, claim descent from Solomon and the Queen of Sheba.

as did another trading city, Djenne, now in Guinea. Mali was later swallowed up by another empire, Songhay, which had been a province of Mali.

On the other side of Africa, the Christian empire of Ethiopia was cut off from the Christians of Europe by the spread of Islam in northern Africa. After Lalibela became emperor in 1190, he moved the capital from Axum (*see* pages 102–103) to a town called Roha, later renamed Lalibela in his honour.

In 1270 Yekuno Amlak seized the throne. His family claimed descent from Solomon and the Queen of Sheba. The very last emperor of Ethiopia, Haile Selassie (who ruled from 1930 to 1974) was a descendant of Yekuno.

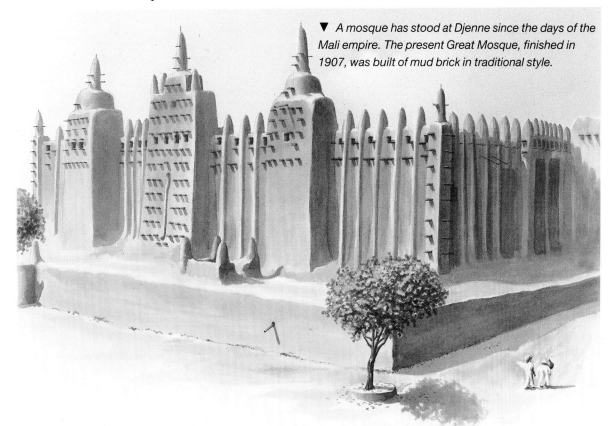

▼ *A mosque has stood at Djenne since the days of the Mali empire. The present Great Mosque, finished in 1907, was built of mud brick in traditional style.*

The Friars

Giovanni Bernadone, son of a cloth merchant from Assisi in central Italy, dreamed of becoming a chivalrous knight. He was known as *Il Francesco*, the little Frenchman, from which came the name Francis. One day he realized that his true vocation (calling) was to follow the teachings of Jesus, give up all his possessions and preach the word of God. So he founded the first order of friars later called the Franciscans or Friars Minor (Little Brothers). He is now known as St Francis of Assisi.

Friars supplied a real need in the medieval world. Nuns and monks in their cloisters had withdrawn from the world in order to worship God. But in the expanding towns, teachers and

▼ *Robes worn by friars showed to which order they belonged. On the far left is a nun. To her right are a Franciscan friar, a Dominican friar, a Carmelite friar and an Augustinian or Austin friar.*

UNIVERSITIES

The University of Bologna in Italy, founded in 1100, is believed to be the oldest university in Europe. Universities were set up to educate priests and monks to a higher level than that found in monastery schools. Many friars taught at them. The Dominicans were a clever and industrious order, but always followed a set doctrine. The Franciscans were more independent thinkers and interested in science. One Franciscan, Alexander of Hales, became a professor at the University of Paris, founded in 1150.

ST FRANCIS

Francis (1182–1226) was born in Assisi, Italy to a wealthy family. He gave up this life in 1205 and devoted himself to the poor and sick. In 1210 he founded the Order of Franciscans. After his death he was made a saint in 1228.

RULES FOR FRIARS

St Francis of Assisi drew up a number of rules for his friars to follow. They were to adopt a life of poverty, owning nothing themselves except the simplest clothes. Friars were to practise strict self-denial, abstaining from all worldly pleasures (Francis himself ate only the plainest food). Above all, each friar was expected to preach the Gospels (in the Bible) to as many people as possible.

1245 Papacy: Pope Innocent IV sends Friar John of Pian del Carpine to explore Mongolia (returns 1249).

1247 Italy: Bitter war between Holy Roman Emperor Frederick II and papal allies (to 1250). Japan: Mongols invade.

1248 The Seventh Crusade begins, led by Louis IX of France (to 1270).

1250 Holy Roman Empire: Conrad IV becomes emperor (to 1254). Seventh Crusade: Saracens capture Louis IX in Egypt, but he is ransomed.

1252 Italy: Golden florins minted at Florence.

1253 France: Louis IX sends Friar William of Rubruquis to Mongolia (returns 1255).

1254 Holy Roman Empire: The Great Interregnum starts. It is a bitter struggle for the imperial crown (to 1273).

1256 Wales: Prince Llewellyn sweeps the English from his country. Papacy: Alexander IV founds the Augustinian Order from several groups of hermits.

This illustration, taken from a medieval manuscript, symbolizes St Francis of Assisi's love of nature as he stands surrounded by birds, a lion and an oak tree.

1258 England: Barons compel Henry III to accept a series of reforms called the Provisions of Oxford.

1260 China: Mongol chief Kublai is elected khan by his army at Shan-tu. Germany: The Hanseatic League is formed.

1261 England: The pope allows Henry III to break his promise to keep the Provisions of Oxford. Papacy: Urban IV becomes pope (to 1264). Byzantine empire: Michael VIII restores Byzantine authority.

preachers could help in the community. The friars lived and worked among the people. They addressed each other as 'brother', and the name friar came from the Latin word for brother, *frater*.

Francis intended that his friars should work for their living, and only beg if they were unable to work. In time friars became so busy teaching that they had no time to earn a living. So begging became their means of survival and they were known as *mendicants* or beggars.

A second order of friars was founded in southern France six years later by Dominic, a Castilian canon from Spain. Its members were called the Dominicans. Other important orders were the Carmelites, founded at Mount Carmel in Palestine, and the Augustinians, or Austin Friars, who followed the teachings of St Augustine of Hippo.

Some friars were known by the colour of their robes. The Franciscans were Grey Friars (though they later wore brown), the Dominicans were Black Friars, and the Carmelites, White Friars.

Food and Farming

In Europe the peasants lived mainly on a diet of bread, cheese and beer. Occasionally they killed one of their pigs and ate its meat. They might also kill an old sheep if it was no longer producing lambs or very good wool. Its meat would be tough, however, and so it would be stewed for a long time to try and make it more tender. Herbs from the garden, together with vegetables and beans, were sometimes added.

In contrast, rich people ate meat or fish. Some meat and fish came from their farms and special fish ponds. Some was hunted, such as swans and herons, as well as deer, rabbits and hares.

Everyone had the problem of getting enough food to last through winter. If the harvest was poor, then the old and the weak could easily starve. Even strong people could die because hunger left them more likely to catch diseases. A great plague swept through Europe in 1347 after a series of bad harvests. Although it was devastating at the time, it led to an improvement in the lives of the survivors.

▲ *Aztec farmers grew vegetables on reed platforms called* chinampas. *These were built in a lake and were covered with fertile mud. The Aztecs also caught birds and fish to eat.*

▼ *About 90 per cent of the people in England lived and worked in the countryside. In spring, they ploughed the land and sowed seeds by hand. As they worked children scared the birds away. Later all the weeds had to be pulled out by hand.*

▶ *The heavy plough made it possible to use the clay soils of central Europe, as well as parts of England. It was pulled by a horse or a team of oxen. Few farmers were rich enough to own their own plough. Often, the plough and the draught animals would be shared by many villagers.*

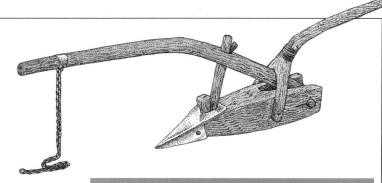

Grapes

Figs

Ginger

Almonds

Spices for preserving meats

WHEN IT HAPPENED

1100 Men returning from the First Crusade bring back spices from the Middle East. They also bring back the knowledge of how to use them for cooking.

1347 The Black Death arrives in Europe and lasts until 1353. Those who survive ask for higher wages and better living conditions.

***c.* 1400** Many land owners turn arable land to sheep pasture as the demand for wool increases.

***c.* 1450** By this date, farmers are practising seed selection to try and improve their crops.

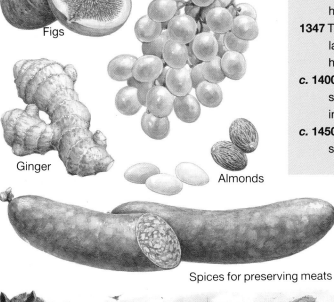

◀ *When the Crusaders came home from the Near East, they brought with them many different sorts of food. These included oranges and lemons, figs, raisins and dates. They also brought sugared almonds at a time when sugar was unknown in most of Europe. Like the Vikings, they also brought back spices which came to the Near East from India and the islands of the Moluccas. These included ginger, cinnamon and pepper. They were used to hide the taste of meat which was going bad or which had been salted to preserve it over the winter. This led to the development of the spice trade. After the fall of the Ottoman empire, Europeans started looking for routes to India and the Moluccas, so they could trade directly with the spice growers.*

1264 England: Simon de Montfort and other English barons defeat Henry III at the battle of Lewes, and take him prisoner. Mongolia: Kublai Khan reunites the Mongol empire. He transfers China's capital to Yen-ching and builds Khanbaliq (modern Beijing) on the sight of the former Chin capital.

1265 England: Simon de Montfort asks leading citizens from the main towns to take part in Parliament. Henry III's son Edward defeats and kills Simon de Montfort at battle of Evesham. Papacy: Clement IV becomes pope (to 1268).

The Mongols moved from place to place by transporting their yurts (tents) on wagons.

1266 English philosopher and scientist Roger Bacon invents the magnifying glass.

1268 Papacy: following the death of Clement IV, the Holy See remains vacant until 1271. Palestine: Muslims from Egypt capture Antioch which had been held by the Christians.

1270 France: Louis IX dies on the Seventh Crusade. He is succeeded by Philip III, the Bold (to 1285). Ethiopia: Yekuno Amlak becomes emperor (to 1285).

1271 Venice: Merchant Marco Polo, his father and his uncle set off to visit the court of Kublai Khan in north China along the Silk Road (return 1295). Papacy: Gregory X becomes pope (to 1276).

1272 England: Edward I is king (to 1307).

1273 Holy Roman Empire: Rudolf I is made emperor (to 1291).

1274 Japan: Kublai Khan's Mongols invade but fail to gain a foothold.

The Mongol Empire

In 1180 a 13-year-old boy suddenly became the leader of his tribe when his father was poisoned. The boy was named Temujin, and his tribe were a warlike nomadic people who lived in Mongolia, the Yakka Mongols. Two-thirds of the tribe promptly deserted him, but very soon Temujin reunited them. He went on to conquer other Mongol tribes. In 1206, a meeting of the *khans* (chiefs of tribes) hailed Temujin as Genghis Khan, 'Emperor of All Men'. He promised that future generations of Mongols would lead lives of luxury.

Genghis Khan began a career of conquest by training a ruthless, well-disciplined army. His hordes terrified their opponents, killing people who did not surrender and often butchering those who did. In a series of brilliant campaigns, Genghis Khan conquered northern China and Korea, then swung westward to overrun northern India, Afghanistan, Persia and parts of Russia.

After Genghis died, his son Ogodai conquered Armenia and Tibet, then

▼ *Mongol horsemen were trained to shoot with bow and arrows while riding at full gallop. In this way they hunted game, and in battle their sharp arrows could pierce an enemy's armour.*

▲ *Mongol sports were designed to train their warriors for war and make them fit. From boyhood on they practised archery and wrestling.*

turned toward Europe, ravaging Hungary and Poland. His nephew, Kublai Khan, completed the conquest of China and made himself emperor of China. He was the first ruler of the Yuan dynasty which held power until 1368.

A Venetian merchant called Marco Polo (*see* pages 282–283) spent 17 years at the court of Kublai Khan. His account of life there showed that the Mongols in China now lived the life of luxury promised them earlier by Genghis.

HOW THE MONGOLS LIVED

The Mongols were wandering herdsmen, roaming over the bleak plains of Mongolia with their cattle and sheep, and riding small, sturdy ponies. They lived in *yurts*, tents made of hides or cloth stretched over a collapsible wooden frame. A hole at the top let out the smoke from the fire. The tents were transported on ox-drawn carts.

It was a male-dominated world: the warriors sat nearest the fire and ate the best food, while the women sat further away and ate what was left. Children had to make do with scraps, or whatever small animals they could catch for themselves.

▼ *In battle Mongol warriors wore helmets of iron or hard leather. Their armour was made of iron plates linked together by strong leather thongs.*

GENGHIS KHAN

1167 Born Temujin.
1206 Becomes Genghis Khan.
1210–14 Conquers northern China.
1218–25 Overruns Persia, Turkestan and Afghanistan.
1227 Dies after a fall.

TAMERLANE

1336 Born in Samarkand.
1370 Becomes ruler of Turkestan.
1383 Conquers Persia.
1391 Occupies Moscow.
1398 Invades India.
1401 Defeats Syria.
1405 Dies in Kazakhstan.

▼ *A charge by the mounted archers and sword-wielding cavalry of the Mongol armies struck fear into any force that opposed them. News of Mongol victories spread throughout Europe and travellers told horrifying tales of their ferocity. The Mongols were said to eat their captives. The Mongol invasion cut off Russia, Asia and the Far East from Europe.*

▲ *The ancient Persian game of polo, played there since the 6th century BC, was adopted by the Mongols because it helped to give their warriors the excellent skills in horsemanship necessary for fighting battles.*

After the death of Kublai Khan in 1294, the mighty Mongol empire that he had tried to rule from Khanbaliq (now Beijing) broke up. But other Mongol khans carved out smaller empires for themselves in central and western Asia, such as Kipchak, which included a large area of Russia. Russians called it the Golden Horde because of the magnificent tent in which its khan lived.

Cruel though the Mongols were, none was as barbarous as the great Mongol chief, Tamerlane (Timur-i-Lenk)sometimes called Timur the Lame

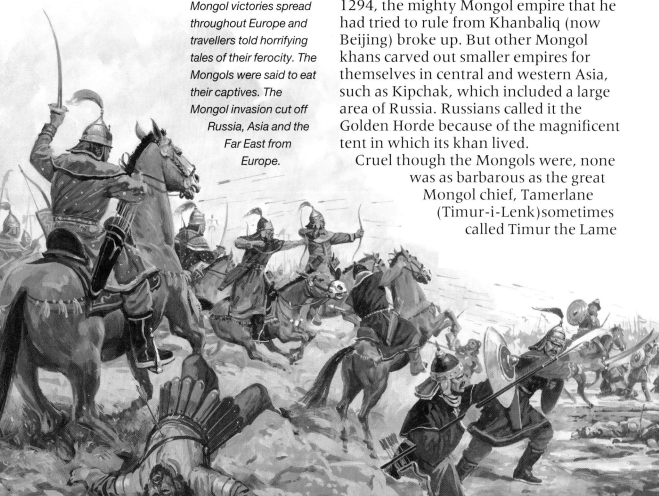

▲ *At its greatest extent in the 13th century during the reign of Kublai Khan, the Mongol empire extended from the Pacific Ocean to the Black Sea.*

because of his battle wounds. He ruled from Samarkand in Turkestan but overran Persia (Iran), Mesopotamia (Iraq), Armenia, Georgia, Azerbaijan and the Golden Horde. For a year he occupied Moscow. He died marching on China. Despite his cruel reputation he was a great patron of the arts and brought many craftsmen to beautify his capital city of Samarkand.

TAMERLANE'S TOMB

When Tamerlane died he was buried in a beautiful jade-covered tomb just outside the city of Samarkand in central Asia. Called Gur Amir, the tomb was finally opened by archaeologists in 1941, and is thought to be one of the finest examples of Islamic art from this period.

1275 China: Marco Polo enters the service of Kublai Khan and travels widely in the Mongol empire during the next 17 years.

1276 Papacy: Innocent V is the first Dominican to become pope. He dies five months after election and is succeeded by Adrian V who dies five weeks after being elected. The successor Pope John XXI dies after eight months in office.

1277 England: Roger Bacon is exiled for heresy (to 1292). Papacy: Nicholas III becomes pope (to 1280).

1278 Holy Roman Empire: Rudolf I defeats and kills Ottakar of Bohemia at battle of the Marchfeld.

A pottery figure of an actor made at the time of the Yuan dynasty, when China was ruled by the Mongols.

1279 Holy Roman Empire: Rudolf I surrenders claims to Sicily and the Papal States. China: Kublai Khan completes the Mongol conquest of the whole of China and founds the Yuan (Mongol) dynasty (to 1368).

1281 Papacy: Martin IV becomes pope (to 1285). Japan: The second Mongol invasion ends in disaster.

1283 Wales: Edward I of England defeats and kills Llewellyn, Prince of Wales, and also executes Llewellyn's brother David. The English conquest of Wales is complete and Edward I orders the building of Caernarvon castle.

1285 France: Philip IV becomes king (to 1314). Papacy: Honorius IV is made pope (to 1287).

1286 Scotland: Margaret, the Maid of Norway, becomes queen, succeeding her grandfather Alexander III (to 1290).

1287 Burma (Myanmar): Mongols pillage Pagan, the capital.

1288 Papacy: Nicholas IV becomes pope (to 1292).

John Balliol reigned in Scotland from 1292 to 1296. Unwillingly, he paid homage to Edward I, King of England and in 1295 he tried to ally himself with France. This led England to invade Scotland. Balliol gave up his throne and retired to his estates in France where he died in 1314.

1289 China: Friar John of Montecorvino becomes the first Christian archbishop of Beijing.

1290 Scotland: Margaret dies; many men claim the Scottish throne. India: Turkish leader Firuz founds the Khalji dynasty (to 1320) in Delhi. England: The Jewish population is expelled.

1291 Scotland: Scots acknowledge Edward I of England as their sovereign; he arbitrates in the succession dispute. Palestine: Saracens (Muslims) capture Acre, the last Christian stronghold in Palestine. Although the Crusades continue, their great age is at an end.

1292 Scotland: Edward I of England nominates John Balliol as king (to 1296). Holy Roman Empire: Adolf, Count of Nassau, emperor (to 1298).

1293 China: First Christian missionaries arrive.

1294 Papacy: Celestine V (the hermit Peter of Morrone) becomes pope but he resigns after five months. Boniface VIII, lawyer, diplomat and believer in the magic arts, becomes pope (to 1303). China: Death of Kublai Khan.

Robert the Bruce

A little girl of three became Queen of Scotland in 1286 when her grandfather, Alexander III, died. She was Margaret, known as the Maid of Norway because her mother was the wife of the King of Norway. She died at sea four years later, on her way to Scotland. There was no obvious heir, and 13 men claimed the throne.

Some of the claimants asked Edward I of England to decide who should rule Scotland. There were two leading contestants, John Balliol and Robert Bruce. Edward chose Balliol, but in 1296 Balliol defied Edward. Edward at once invaded Scotland and ruled himself.

Many Scots resented this treatment. In 1297 a Scottish knight, William Wallace, led a rebellion. It was crushed and

▼ *Robert I was born in 1274. He was enthroned at Scone, near Perth, as were all Scottish kings. Robert died in 1329 and was succeeded by his son, David II.*

THE SPIDER'S LESSON

Legend says that Robert the Bruce, in despair after a defeat, was sheltering in a cave when he saw a spider trying again and again to climb a thread. Eventually it succeeded and Bruce decided never to give up the fight.

SCOTTISH CLAIMANTS TO THE THRONE

The question of the Scottish succession (who has the right to rule) was a complicated one and it was made worse by the number of claimants to the throne after Margaret, the Maid of Norway, died.

Alexander III was the direct descendant in the male line of the first ruler of a united Scotland, Duncan I (1034–1040). John Balliol and Robert Bruce were both very distant cousins of Alexander, being descended through the female line from David, Earl of Huntingdon, the younger brother of Alexander III's grandfather, King William 'the Lion'.

Robert I's son David II had no children, so the throne descended through Robert's daughter Marjorie, who married Walter Fitzalan, High Steward of Scotland. His position gave the family its name, the house of Stuart. Robert II became the first Stuart king of Scotland.

Wallace was beheaded, but a new champion appeared: Robert Bruce's grandson, who was also named Robert and is known as Robert the Bruce.

Bruce was ruthless. He and his followers killed his only rival, John Comyn, Balliol's nephew. Bruce began a fresh rebellion. He suffered several defeats, but was saved when Edward I died on his way to subdue Scotland again. Edward's son, Edward II, did not have his father's iron will and Bruce defeated him in 1314 at the battle of Bannockburn. In 1328 Scotland finally became independent from England and Bruce was crowned King Robert I.

▶ The Great Seal of John Balliol, King of Scotland, showing him on horseback.

▼ At the battle of Bannockburn, a Scottish army of about 7000 defeated an English force three times the size.

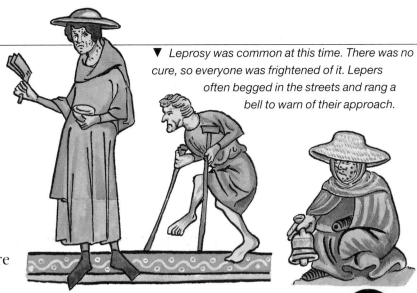

▼ *Leprosy was common at this time. There was no cure, so everyone was frightened of it. Lepers often begged in the streets and rang a bell to warn of their approach.*

People

Life was harsh for poor people in Europe. Many died as babies, but if they survived to the age of 12, they were thought to be adults. They might live to be 60, if they were lucky. People did not know where diseases came from and many died of plagues, smallpox and influenza. Even a small cut could be fatal because no one knew how to keep wounds clean.

The poor spent most of their time working or begging for food. The rich were entertained by singers, dancers and musicians at home. Acrobats and bear-trainers performed in the streets.

▶ *Japanese women always used white make-up on their faces, but this made their teeth look yellow. To hide this, the women painted their teeth black.*

▼ *An illustration of a Chinese Song dynasty tomb painting. It shows a wealthy couple at their table, waited on by four servants. At this time China was the wealthiest and best run state in the world.*

▼ *A Japanese court lady in her underclothes. Over them she wore several silk kimonos.*

▲ European women wore very little make-up. Instead, they plucked their eyebrows and pinned their hair back tightly. It was also fashionable to pluck the forehead.

▼ The clothes people wore showed where they belonged in society. Peasants (left and below) were not allowed to wear scarlet and certain shades of blue or green. Workmen used a certain kind of cloth, friars used another kind and servants made their clothes from cloth with a striped band. Only the rich (right) could afford to be fashionable. Both men and women wore two tunics: a close-fitting one underneath, with a heavier, flowing coat over the top, usually in different colours. Women in northern Europe wore a wimple, a headdress which framed the face.

▲ People played games that we still have today. These included chess, bowls, cards and hide-and-seek. They also played football.

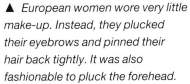

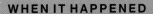
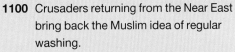

WHEN IT HAPPENED

1100 Crusaders returning from the Near East bring back the Muslim idea of regular washing.

1381 English peasants, led by Wat Tyler, march on London to demand better working conditions.

15th century Illuminated manuscripts such as the Duke of Berry's *The Very Rich Hours* depicting everyday life, are made.

Aztecs and Incas

Two great civilizations were founded within a hundred years or so of each other: the Inca empire in Peru and the Aztec empire in Mexico. According to tradition, Manco Capac and his sister, Mama Ocllo, were the first rulers of the Incas around 1200. They called themselves 'the Children of the Sun' and, if they existed at all, they were probably the leaders of a wandering tribe. Little is known about the emperors who followed except Pachacuti, who succeeded in 1438 and was a brilliant general. He conquered neighbouring tribes and founded the Inca empire.

▲ The location of the Aztec and Inca empires.

▼ The Inca ruler Pachacuti leads his army into battle. Inca soldiers used slings, bolas which were stones linked by lengths of string, wooden spears and swords, and star-shaped clubs.

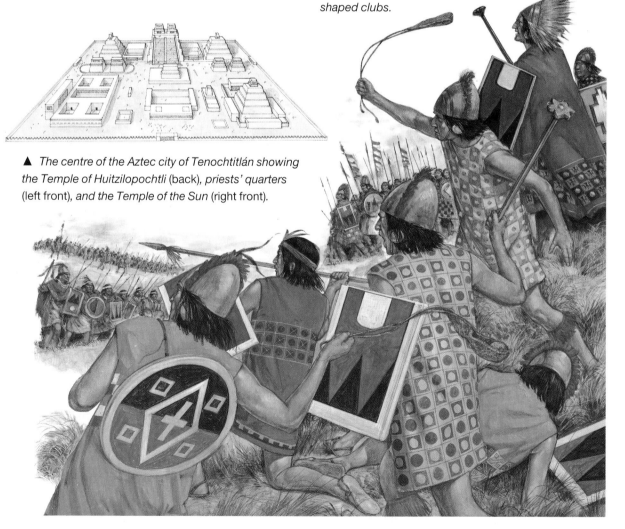

▲ The centre of the Aztec city of Tenochtitlán showing the Temple of Huitzilopochtli (back), priests' quarters (left front), and the Temple of the Sun (right front).

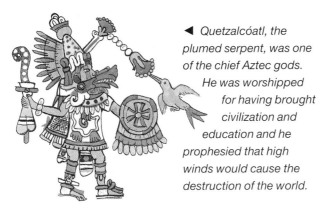

◀ *Quetzalcóatl, the plumed serpent, was one of the chief Aztec gods. He was worshipped for having brought civilization and education and he prophesied that high winds would cause the destruction of the world.*

The Incas probably looked very like their descendants, the Quechua Indians, who live in the highlands of Peru today. Short and stocky, with straight black hair, they are well adapted to life in the thin air of the mountains.

Legends say the Aztecs came from northern Mexico. In 1168, on the instructions of their god Huitzilopochtli, they began to migrate. They eventually settled in the valley of Mexico. In 1325 the Aztecs started to build a city, Tenochtitlán, on an island in Lake Texcoco which is now the site of Mexico City. In the 15th century they went on to conquer the other cities of the valley, and founded the Aztec empire.

AMERICAN FOOD

The Incas mainly lived on potatoes and bred ducks and guinea pigs for eating. Aztecs hunted for fish and birds and bred turkeys. The Aztecs made a chocolate drink from cocoa beans (the tree, pod and beans of cocoa are shown here). Both peoples grew maize (corn), chillies, tomatoes, peanuts, avocados and beans. The Incas made beer from maize.

1295 England: Knights and burgesses from English shires and towns are summoned to the Model Parliament of Edward I. China: Temur Oljaitu (Ch'eng Tsung), grandson of Kublai Khan, becomes emperor of China (to 1307). He is the last effective ruler of the Yuan dynasty.

1296 Scotland: Edward I of England deposes John Balliol. France: Conflict between Philip IV and Pope Boniface VIII over papal powers in France (to 1303).

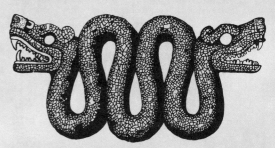

The Aztec god Huitzilopochtli was depicted as a snake. This image is made of wood covered with turquoise. It was probably worn on the back of the head as part of a headdress.

1297 Scotland: Rebellion against the English led by William Wallace. He defeats an English army at the battle of Stirling.

1298 Scotland: Edward I of England defeats Wallace at the battle of Falkirk and reconquers Scotland. Holy Roman Empire: German barons depose Emperor Adolf and elect Albert I (to 1308).

c. **1299** Turkey: Osman I founds the Ottoman empire.

1300 Italy: Bologna University appoints Dorotea Bocchi to succeed her father as professor of medicine, and Maria di Novella as professor and head of mathematics. Peru: Incas begin a period of expansion.

14th century Polynesia: A second wave of Maoris arrive in New Zealand from the Marquesas.

1301 Wales: Edward I of England invests his baby son, Edward, as prince of Wales. Byzantine empire: Osman, founder of the Ottoman Turks, defeats the Byzantines.

Benin and Zimbabwe

The modern country of Benin, formerly called Dahomey, took its name from one of the most powerful empires of West Africa. Called Benin, this empire was situated in eastern Nigeria. Its capital, Benin City, was founded in about AD 900. At its most prosperous in the 15th century, the city had walls 40 kilometres long and wide streets, lined with large wooden houses. The palace of the *oba* (king) was richly decorated with bronze plaques.

The city stood on a major trade route, and its merchants dealt in cloth, ivory, metals (especially bronze), palm oil and pepper. It was the custom for warring black African states to make their prisoners slaves so when the Portuguese reached Benin in the 15th century (*see* pages 306–307), they took advantage of this and bought slaves. The slave trade became one of Benin's greatest sources of money. Benin reached its height during the reign of Oba Ewuare the Great, who ruled from 1440 to 1481.

Benin is renowned for its art, especially

▲ *This Benin bronze shows an oba seated on his throne, with two subjects kneeling beside him. Benin craftsmen cast bronzes by the 'lost wax' process. A mould is made by covering a wax model with clay, then the wax is melted away and molten bronze poured in.*

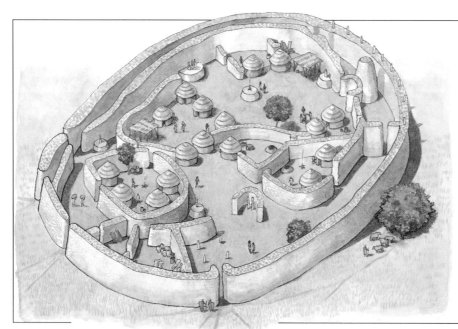

GREAT ZIMBABWE

One of the greatest African mysteries is the walled city of Great Zimbabwe, after which modern Zimbabwe is named. The massive stone ruins were built of granite blocks from the 11th to the 14th centuries, but nobody knows why or by whom. Great Zimbabwe appears to have been a centre for religion and the gold trade.

◄ *This lifelike ivory mask shows an oba of Benin. The oba hung it round his waist on ceremonial occasions. This particular sculpture must have been made after Portuguese explorers began visiting the area in the 15th century, because the headdress depicts a row of Portuguese sailors. According to a traditional Benin belief, wearing representations of strangers in this way enabled the oba to 'take over' the newcomers.*

the bronze and ivory sculptures of the heads of its rulers and their wives. But there was a darker side to the empire: although the people were friendly to strangers, there existed a tradition of human sacrifice which later earned Benin City the name 'City of Blood'.

▼ *Some African civilizations during the Middle Ages.*

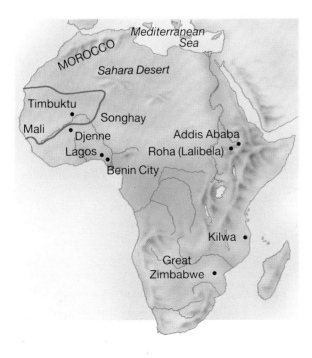

1302 Flanders: The Flemish defeat the best French soldiers at the battle of Courtrai and save their country from French occupation. Papacy: A decree called *Unam Sanctam* declares papal authority to be supreme.

1303 Papacy: Guillaume de Nogaret, emissary of Philip IV of France, captures Pope Boniface VIII at Anagni, Italy, and ill-treats him. The pope is rescued by the citizens of Anagni, but dies soon after. Benedict XI becomes pope (to 1304).

1305 Scotland: The English capture and execute William Wallace. Papacy: Clement V (Bertrand de Got, Archbishop of Bordeaux) is made pope (to 1314).

1306 Scotland: Robert Bruce leads a rebellion against English rule. He is crowned Robert I (to 1329) at Scone.

A 14th century bronze head of an oni, or king, of Ife, a kingdom in what is now Nigeria. He is wearing the headdress of a sea god. This sculpture has been called one of the finest surviving sculptures of medieval African art.

1307 Africa: Mansa Musa is made king of Mali (to 1337). Around the same time Benin emerges as an empire in West Africa. England: Edward I dies marching north to crush Robert of Scotland: his son Edward II becomes king (to 1327).

1308 Holy Roman Empire: Henry VII becomes emperor (to 1313).

1309 Pope Clement V transfers the papal see (capital) from Rome to Avignon, France; it remains there until 1377.

1310 England: The barons appoint 21 peers, known as the Lords Ordainers, to manage Edward II's household.

1312 Order of Knights Templars is abolished for malpractices, such as dishonesty in business and heresy.

Medieval Explorers

Many bold men made long, and often dangerous, journeys in the Middle Ages. The first good account of central Asia was written by a Franciscan friar, John of Pian del Carpine, who was sent on a mission in 1245 to the Great Khan of Mongolia by Pope Innocent IV. Another 'official' traveller was the Chinese admiral, Zheng He. Between 1405 and 1433, he led seven naval expeditions to extend China's political influence over maritime Asia. He returned with many luxuries such as spices.

Trade was the reason for many of these journeys. The greatest European traveller was Marco Polo, a young Venetian

▼ The incredible journeys of medieval travellers covered thousands of miles. Many suffered hardships such as frostbite, but others enjoyed luxury.

▲ The first giraffe seen in China was brought back from Africa by Admiral Zheng He. It had its portrait painted by order of the emperor.

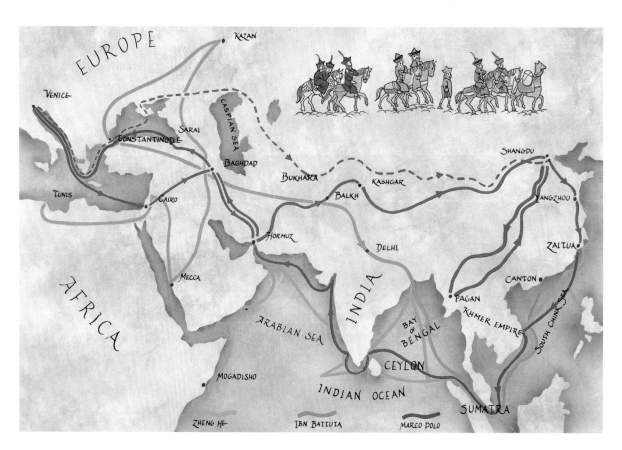

MARCO POLO

Marco Polo (1254–1324), his father and uncle took three years to reach China in 1275. In 1284 Marco became China's envoy to India. His return to Venice in 1295, sparked great interest in the East.

IBN BATTUTA

Ibn Battuta (1304–1368) left Tangier on a pilgrimage to Mecca in 1325. He went on to visit East Africa, India via Russia, and China before returning home in 1349. Finally he toured West Africa.

merchant. He travelled to the court of Kublai Khan in China and worked there for many years. Returning in 1295 laden with jewels, he later composed a vivid account of his travels. But the greatest travellers at this time were the Arabs. Ibn Battuta, a Moroccan lawyer, visited Russia, India and Africa and left a detailed description of his travels.

▼ *Huge ships like this one were specially built for Zheng He's expeditions; 62 sailed on his first voyage.*

1314 Scotland: Edward II of England invades but Robert I defeats him at the battle of Bannockburn. France: Louis X, the Quarrelsome, becomes king (to 1316). Holy Roman Empire: Louis IV becomes emperor (to 1347): civil war follows with his rival, Frederick of Austria.

1316 France: Philip V, the Tall, is made king (to 1322). Papacy: John XXII becomes pope (to 1334): the papacy sends eight Dominican friars to Ethiopia in search of Prester John, a legendary Christian leader.

1317 France: Women are excluded from succeeding to the French throne, through the Salic Law.

1320 India: Tughluk dynasty in Delhi (to 1413), is founded by the Turk Ghidyas-ud-din Tughluk. He encourages agriculture, reforms taxes and creates a postal system.

A mask of the demon Hannya. It was used in the Japanese Nō theatre. Developed in the 14th century, Nō plays are still performed in Japan today. All the actors are men and very little scenery is used.

1322 France: Charles IV, the Fair becomes king (to 1328).

1323 Flanders: Peasants' revolt begins. It is eventually suppressed by the French army in 1328.

1324 Mansa Musa, King of Mali, travels to Mecca. The magnificence of his court astonishes all who see him.

1325 Mexico: Traditional date when Tenochtitlán (now Mexico City) is founded by the Aztecs. Arabia: Ibn Battuta begins his tours of Mecca, India and Africa. Later he records his 30 years of travel in the book Rihla (journey).

Religion

Fighting between Christians and Muslims broke out in the Near East because they both shared the same holy places. People of all religions had been allowed to visit peacefully until the Seljuk Turks refused to let Christians visit Jerusalem. The Christians tried to recapture the city in a series of Crusades. In Europe, many Christians went on pilgrimages. If they could not go, they paid people called palmers to go in their place.

Meanwhile, the Arabs continued to spread the Islamic faith across Africa until Ethiopia was the only Christian country left in northern Africa. Muslims, too, went on pilgrimages, but their destination was Mecca.

In Asia Buddhism, spread by missionaries, was split into many branches as it combined with many local beliefs.

◀ Louis IX, King of France (1226–1270), was a deeply religious man. He vowed he would go on Crusade if he recovered from a dangerous illness, which he did and in 1248 he led the Seventh Crusade against Egypt. He was killed in 1270 on Crusade in Tunis, North Africa. He was thought of as the ideal ruler, even his enemies respected him for his fairness and in 1297 he was made a saint.

▼ This Buddhist wisdom text was written on a palm leaf in 1112. It is written in Sanskrit, an ancient Indian language used by Buddhists and Hindus all over India. Buddhism and Hinduism were the main religions in India at this time.

▲ During the twelfth century, Zen, a branch of Buddhism, spread to Japan from China. Its strict code appealed to Japanese warriors, the samurai. Buddhist temple buildings, such as this gateway, were also built in the Chinese style.

► *The remains of the mosque at Kilwa, East Africa, founded by Arab traders. Trade spread the Muslim faith throughout Africa.*

▼ *Reliquaries contained holy relics and the bones of saints. People made long journeys to see them.*

WHEN IT HAPPENED

1204 The Crusaders seize Constantinople.

1209 St Francis of Assisi starts the Franciscan order of friars.

1345 The Aztecs arrive in Central Mexico. Their religion includes human sacrifice.

1453 Constantinople falls to the Ottoman Turks who convert the great Christian church of St Sophia into a mosque.

▼ *Early medieval churches had no furniture. People stood during services, but there were special ledges for old people to lean on.*

1326 England: Queen Isabella, Edward II's wife, and her lover Roger Mortimer sail from France with an army to lead a rebellion against Edward. Turkey: Orkhan I becomes the first real ruler and organizer of the Ottoman Turks (to 1359). The Ottomans capture the city of Bursa, Anatolia.

1327 England: Parliament declares Edward II deposed, and his son becomes Edward III. Edward II is murdered nine months later. Holy Roman Empire: Emperor Louis IV invades Italy and declares Pope John XXII deposed.

In medieval Europe pedlars travelled from door to door to display their wares. Here a woman inspects the goods, hung up outside her home. Pedlars also acted as a means of spreading news and stories.

1328 England acknowledges Scotland's independence. France: Philip VI becomes king (to 1350), the first French ruler of the house of Valois.

1329 Scotland: five-year-old David II ascends the throne (to 1371).

1332 Scotland: Edward Balliol, son of John Balliol, attempts to seize the Scottish throne but he is defeated and flees over the border to England.

1333 Scotland: Edward III invades Scotland on Edward Balliol's behalf and defeats the Scots. Japan: Emperor Daigo II overthrows the Hojo family of shoguns and rules himself (to 1336).

1334 Papacy: Benedict XII becomes pope (to 1342).

1336 Japan: Daigo II is exiled. Ashikaga family rule Japan as shoguns (to 1573); civil war starts (to 1392).

1337 Edward III of England declares himself king of France starting the Hundred Years War (to 1453).

The Hundred Years War

The Hundred Years War between England and France was not one long war, but a series of short ones. It began in 1337 and ended in 1453, so the conflict actually lasted for 116 years. English kings tried to dominate France, while the French strove to throw the English out of their country.

In 1328 Charles IV of France died without a direct heir. French barons gave the throne to his cousin, Philip VI, but Charles's nephew, Edward III of England, challenged him. When Philip declared that Edward's French lands were confiscated, war broke out.

The English defeated a French fleet in the English Channel at Sluys, then invaded France and won a major land battle at Crécy. Edward then captured Calais. But both sides ran out of money and had to agree a truce, which lasted from 1347 until 1355.

In 1355 a fresh English invasion took place, led by Edward's heir, Edward, whose nickname was 'the Black Prince'. The Black Prince won a resounding victory at Poitiers, capturing Philip's successor, John II. The Treaty of Brétigny in 1360 gave England large parts of France. But a new campaign followed the peace treaty and England lost most of her French possessions.

For a while both the French and English thrones were occupied by children, Charles VI of France and Richard II of England. Richard's uncle, John of Gaunt (Ghent), Duke of Lancaster, ruled for him. In 1396 Richard II married Charles VI's daughter, Isabelle, and a 20-year truce was agreed.

▶ *At the battle of Crécy in 1346 an English army of 10,000 men defeated a French force of 20,000. The English archers easily outshot the French crossbows. Over 1500 French died, but only 40 English.*

WEAPONRY

The longbow *(left)*, made of yew, was developed in England during the 13th century. English archers could fire six carefully aimed arrows a minute, each a 'cloth-yard' (1 metre) long. They were accurate at a range of up to 320 metres.

French archers and other European soldiers used the crossbow *(right)*. Its bolts (missiles) did not carry as far as the longbow's arrows. It was easier to fire than a longbow, but much slower.

JOHN OF GAUNT

John of Gaunt (1340–1399), born at Ghent, was one of the sons of Edward III. In 1372 he claimed the throne of Castile through his wife. As regent (1377–1386) for Richard II he was the most powerful man in England.

▶ *Edward, Prince of Wales, got his nickname the Black Prince from the colour of his armour.*

1338 Holy Roman Empire: Electors of the empire declare it to be independent from the papacy. The Treaty of Coblenz forms an alliance between England and the empire.

1340 Hundred Years War: A naval victory at Sluys gives England the command of the English Channel. England: Parliament passes four statutes providing that taxation shall be imposed only by Parliament.

Gold florins from Florence had a lily on one side and St John the Baptist on the other.

1341 Mali: Sulaiman becomes king (to 1360).

1342 Papacy: Clement VI is made pope (to 1352).

1344 Germany: By now almost all larger German towns along the Baltic and North seas belong to the Hanseatic League.

1345 Ottoman Turks first cross the Bosporus into Europe.

1346 Hundred Years War: Edward III of England invades France and defeats a large army under Philip VI at the battle of Crécy. Scotland: David II of Scotland is defeated and captured by the English. Serbia: Stephen Dushan, King of the Serbs, is crowned 'Emperor of the Serbs and Greeks'.

1347 Hundred Years War: The English capture Calais. Holy Roman Empire: Charles IV becomes emperor (to 1378). Italy: Patriot Cola da Rienzi assumes power in Rome, taking the title of 'tribune', but he is soon driven from office. The Black Death reaches Genoa from Central Asia.

The Hanseatic League

Trade routes in the late Middle Ages were often threatened by pirates at sea and robbers on land. In 1241 two north German towns, Hamburg and Lübeck, agreed to protect each other's merchants by setting up a *hansa* or trading association. Two groups of traders formed the Hanseatic League in 1260. North German merchants based in Lübeck had a virtual monopoly (sole rights) of trade around the Baltic Sea, while merchants based in Cologne and other Rhine cities traded with England and the Low Countries (now Belgium and the Netherlands).

The Hanseatic League brought food and raw materials from eastern Europe in exchange for manufactured goods from the west. From Russia and lands to the south and east of the Baltic, Hanse ships carried charcoal, flax, grain, hemp (rope), honey, pitch and timber. Hanse merchants secured a monopoly of Norwegian cod and whale oil, and Swedish iron mines and herrings. They also traded overland to Venice and Constantinople (now Istanbul).

NOVGOROD

The fortified city of Novgorod, in western Russia, was the farthest into Russia Hanse merchants reached. Novgorod traded in amber, furs and wax.

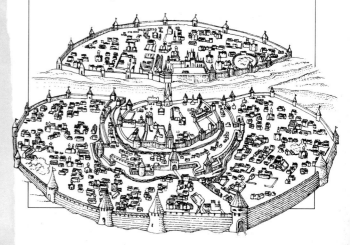

THE KONTORE

The Hanseatic League had depots, called *kontore*, in some countries. In Bergen, Bruges, London and Novgorod, the kontore obeyed the laws of the League rather than those of the countries they were in. Traders in London were called 'Merchants of the Steelyard' from the old German word *stalhof* (a yard used for displaying samples).

The Hanse towns safeguarded their ships with lighthouses and they fought off pirates at sea. The League also took political action to safeguard its monopolies. Member towns were forbidden to fight each other and highway robbery was put at an end. If other countries or towns would not co-operate, it forced them to do so by applying financial pressure.

▲ *When it was at its peak, the main trading routes of the Hanseatic League covered Europe. The League began to collapse in the early 17th century.*

▼ *It was in small, sturdy ships like these that the goods of the Hanseatic merchants were carried. Western cloth, linen, silverware and wool were exchanged for eastern spices, silk and raw materials.*

The Black Death

The Black Death is sometimes said to have been the worst disaster in history. It killed about 25 million people in Europe alone (about a quarter of the total population), and nobody knows how many millions more in Asia.

The Black Death was a form of bubonic plague. It got its name from spots of blood that formed under the skin and turned black. The first symptoms were the swelling of glands in the groin and armpit. Victims usually died within a few hours. The plague was first carried by rat fleas which could also live on humans. Bubonic plague is not carried by human contact, but the Black Death later changed to pneumonic plague, which spreads from person to person.

The disease seems to have been carried from central Asia to the Crimea by a Tartar (Mongol) raiding party, and from there to the Mediterranean by ship, arriving at Genoa, in Italy, in 1347. It

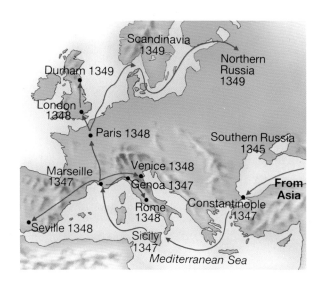

▲ The Black Death came from Asia to Europe in 1347 and reached its peak in 1349. Only a few areas were unaffected because people managed to isolate themselves and stop the disease from spreading.

▼ A typical European town street in the Middle Ages had filthy open sewers, rats and refuse everywhere. Human waste was hurled from the windows with the cry 'Gardez-loo!' to warn passers-by. It was no wonder the plague spread, but many people thought it was the judgment of God on a wicked world.

▲ *The feelings of fear and helplessness were reflected in the art and literature of the time. Pictures showed the Black Death as a skeleton riding on horseback.*

spread west and north, reaching Paris and London in 1348, and Scandinavia and northern Russia in 1349. It devastated regions: houses stood empty and towns were abandoned. Fields became littered with unburied corpses.

The effects of the Black Death were widespread. Before it, Europe had had a surplus of labour and wages were low. Afterwards there was a severe shortage of workers. As a result wages soared and attempts to hold wages down led to revolts (*see* pages 62–63). The already weak feudal system collapsed.

▼ *People burned the clothes of the dead to try to stop the infection spreading. The plague killed rich and poor alike and sometimes whole towns were wiped out.*

1348 England: Edward III establishes the Order of the Garter. The Black Death ravages Europe, reaching Paris and London. In England it kills about one third of the population.

1348–1353 Italy: The poet Boccaccio writes the *Decameron* which is about ten young people who leave Florence to escape the plague and tell each other tales for ten days.

1349 The Black Death reaches northern Russia. Spain: Pedro the Cruel becomes king of Castile (to 1369). Holy Roman Empire: The Jews are persecuted.

1350 France: John II becomes king (to 1364).

The Black Death, which wiped out over one third of the population of Europe, was spread by fleas which lived on rats. The rats made their nests in houses and so infected humans.

1352 Mali: Ibn Battuta spends time here after exploring the Sahara. China: The Black Death arrives.

1354 Italy: Rienzi returns to power in Rome and is killed by his opponents.

1356 Hundred Years War: Edward the Black Prince, son of Edward III, defeats the French at the battle of Poitiers, and captures the French king John II.

1358 France: A revolt by the peasants is suppressed by the Regent Charles, son of John II.

1360 Hundred Years War: Treaty of Brétigny ends the first stage of the war; Edward III of England gives up his claim to the throne of France. France: The first francs are coined.

1363 Burgundy: Philip the Bold, son of John II, is duke of Burgundy. Mongol leader Tamerlane begins the conquest of Asia.

1364 France: Charles V, the Wise, becomes king (to 1380), on the death of his father, John II, in captivity in London.

Science and Technology

Both the Chinese and the Arabs were still ahead of the rest of the world in science and technology. Crusaders returning to Europe from Palestine carried Arabic knowledge of astronomy and mathematics. Ideas from classical Greek medicine were also introduced.

Knowledge of how to make paper also spread to Europe from Arabia during this period. Along with the development of printing, this made books more plentiful, although most people could not read.

More knowledge from ancient Greece came to Europe after the fall of the Byzantine empire, when many scholars fled from Constantinople to Italy. It was this knowledge which led to the new interest in learning which swept through Europe in the 15th and 16th centuries.

▶ The padded horse collar was originally invented in China. It was introduced into Europe in the 11th century and became widely used by the 12th century. It enabled horses to pull heavy weights, such as ploughs and carts, without the risk of choking themselves as they had sometimes done in the past.

▲ Muslim scholars studying in the library at Hulwan, near Baghdad. Islam preserved many important scientific manuscripts from ancient Greece which would otherwise have been lost.

◀ This servant is washing dishes in a castle kitchen. Diseases were common because no-one understood the connection between dirt and disease.

▲ This stone shows the Aztec 20-day month. They had 18 months plus a final five unlucky days.

▲ Spectacles for long-sighted people were first worn in about 1285. Those for short-sighted people were invented around 1430.

▶ Water wheels were used to power hammers for iron working. This made metal working easier.

▼ Monks knew how to distil alcohol from wine. It was called *aqua vitae*. Fermented cereals were used to make whisky.

WHEN IT HAPPENED

1147 *Al-jebr*, Arabic algebra work, is translated into Latin.

1202 Leonardo Fibonacci, Italian mathematican, writes about the Hindu-Arabic numbering system.

1260 Roger Bacon, English scientist, describes the laws of reflection and refraction.

1266 Bacon invents the magnifying glass.

1275 First known human dissection carried out.

The Ming Dynasty

After the death of Kublai Khan in 1294, the Yuan (Mongol) dynasty of China had a succession of relatively feeble emperors. The last Yuan emperor, Sun Ti, was a bad ruler. The Chinese people were tired of being ruled harshly by foreigners. They found a Chinese ruler in Chu Yuen-Chang, who had been a monk and a beggar. He was a bandit chief, so he had a ready-made army. He also proved to be an excellent general.

After a 13-year campaign he captured Beijing, drove the Mongols back to Mongolia, and became emperor. He founded a new dynasty called the Ming, which means 'brightness', and took the name Hung Wu, which means 'very warlike'. He moved the capital to the fortified city of Nanjing.

Hung Wu ruled China for 30 years as a dictator, but he restored order and prosperity to his land. Any minister who opposed him was executed. The many

THE CIVIL SERVICE

The emperor Hung Wu set up colleges for the sons of public officials; other boys were allowed in if they showed promise. The ambition of every scholar was to obtain one of the 100,000 civil service posts or a post in the 80,000-strong military service. Candidates had to pass examinations in literature and philosophy.
Civil servants had little real power, which lay in the hands of the emperor and the court favourites. However, Ming officials adorned many fine jade carvings of the period.

THE FORBIDDEN CITY

The Ming emperors were great builders. Their masterpiece was Beijing. The two main cities, the Outer and the Inner, were linked by the Tiananmen (Gate of Heavenly Peace). Inside the Inner City was the Imperial City, and inside that, the Forbidden City. It was 'forbidden' because it was built for one man, the emperor, and only his household was allowed into it.

CRAFTS

The Ming period is famous for its blue-and-white porcelain. Some of the porcelain made during Yung Lo's reign is of eggshell thinness. The centre of porcelain manufacture was at Jingdezhen, south of Nanjing, where there is a good supply of clay. Ming craft workers also made enamelware, carpets, carvings and exquisite embroideries.

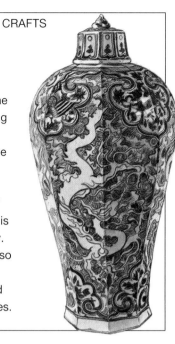

soldiers who had fought in the long civil wars were made farmers, especially on land along the frontier where the Mongols might counter-attack. Hung Wu left the throne to a young grandson, Hui Ti, but Hui Ti was soon overthrown by his uncle, who became the third Ming emperor with the title of Yung Lo. Yung Lo moved the capital back to Beijing, where he built an imperial city.

▼ *A later plan of Beijing, first built in 1410.*

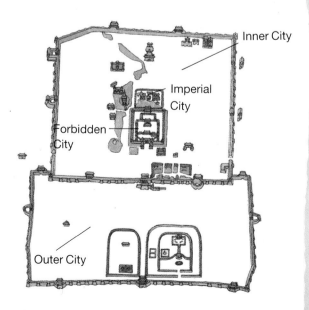

Inner City

Imperial City

Forbidden City

Outer City

1365 Turks make Adrianople their capital.
1367 Confederation of Cologne: 77 Hanse towns prepare for a struggle with Denmark.
1368 China: Rebellion led by Chu Yuen-Chang overthrows the Yuan dynasty and founds the Ming dynasty (to 1644).
1369 Hundred Years War: Second stage of conflict between England and France begins. China: Korea submits to the Ming dynasty. Central Asia: Tamerlane becomes king of Samarkand.

Kublai Khan founded the observatory at Beijing in the 13th century to observe important planetary events. China had a special government astronomy department.

1369 Ottoman Turks begin conquest of Bulgaria (completed 1372).
1370 Hundred Years War: Edward the Black Prince of England sacks Limoges. Holy Roman Empire: Peace of Stralsund establishes the power of the Hanseatic League over the Danish. Papacy: Gregory XI becomes pope (to 1378). Turkestan: Tamerlane becomes ruler.
1371 Scotland: Robert II becomes king (to 1390), the first Stuart monarch. Balkans: Ottoman Turks defeat Serbs, and conquer Macedonia. Spain: John of Gaunt, Duke of Lancaster, younger son of Edward III of England, marries Constance, daughter and heiress of the King of Castile and Leon. John lays claim to the throne of Castile.

1372 Hundred Years War: French troops recapture Poitou and Brittany; naval battle of La Rochelle gives the French control of the English Channel again.

1373 Hundred Years War: John of Gaunt leads a new English invasion of France.

1374 John of Gaunt returns to England and takes charge of the government.

1375 Hundred Years War: Truce of Bruges halts hostilities between England and France. Papacy: Catherine of Siena negotiates the return of the papacy from Avignon to Rome.

A pardoner was an agent of the Church who was licensed to sell indulgences. These documents forgave people the sins they had committed and eased their consciences. They were sold to raise money for the Church.

1376 England: The Good Parliament, called by Edward the Black Prince, introduces many reforms. Later in the same year the Black Prince dies. John Wycliffe, an Oxford University teacher, calls for Church reforms.

1377 England: Acts of the Good Parliament are reversed. Edward III dies. Richard II, son of the Black Prince, is made king (to 1399). Papacy: Pope Gregory XI returns the papal see to Rome.

1378 The Great Schism (to 1417): rival popes are elected: Urban VI, pope at Rome (to 1389), Clement VII, antipope at Avignon (to 1394). Holy Roman Empire: Wenceslas IV becomes emperor (to 1400).

The Great Schism

In the late 14th century, the Christian Church underwent a split, known as the Great Schism. For a short time there were three popes at one time.

In the Middle Ages, the Roman Catholic Church was the only Christian Church in western Europe. The pope was head of a state in Italy as well as a spiritual leader. But at this time Italy was torn by feuds and wars, so in 1309 Pope Clement V, a Frenchman, moved the papal headquarters to Avignon, in southern France. For many years his successors were Frenchmen, and the papacy remained in Avignon until 1377, when Gregory XI decided that it would be better to go back to Rome.

The next year Gregory XI died and under pressure from a group in Rome the cardinals elected an Italian pope, Urban VI. But Urban so upset the cardinals that 13 of them rebelled and elected a Swiss cardinal, Robert of Geneva instead. The two popes each had their own College of Cardinals and claimed to be head of the Church. Some

CHURCH REFORM

The first great English leader of Church reform, John Wycliffe (c. 1320–1384), was a professor of theology at Oxford University. He denounced the corruption and wealth of the Church and its involvement in politics, and began to question some of its basic beliefs. He was supported by the king.

▲ *The French Palace of the Popes stands on a hill in the middle of Avignon, a city in south-eastern France. The palace is also a fortress. It was begun in 1314 and not finished until 1370.*

kings supported one, some the other.

In 1409 a council of churchmen meeting at Pisa in Italy declared both the current popes deposed and elected another. There were now three popes. This was too much and in 1417 another council elected Martin V as the only rightful pope. The Great Schism was finally over. The popes elected in Rome were regarded as the rightful ones. The others were called antipopes.

▲ *In the Middle Ages St Peter's, the church of the popes in Rome, looked like this. Constructed in about 325, it was based on a Roman basilica (meeting hall). St Peter's had slender walls and a light wooden roof. It was demolished in 1506.*

▼ *Europe during the Great Schism. The rulers of Aragon, Castile, France, Navarre, Portugal (to 1381) Savoy and Scotland supported Avignon; England, Flanders, the Holy Roman Empire, Hungary, Italy, Poland and Portugal (from 1381) supported Rome.*

LIFESTYLE OF POPES

The popes and the College of Cardinals who elected them, enjoyed a luxurious lifestyle. The Church's leaders lived in palaces and had many servants to wait on them. The popes headed a large administration. Some of them were more concerned with power and prestige than with spiritual matters.

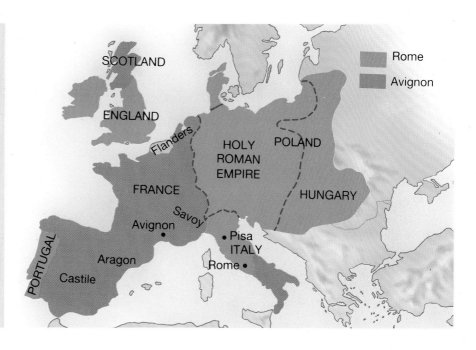

The Peasants' Revolts

After the Black Death killed over a third of the people in Europe, there was a great shortage of labour. Many peasants, labourers and smallholders secured higher wages. But there were more wars, and the cost of maintaining armies soared. As a result, people had to pay more taxes.

Most peasants lived in great poverty. They ate mainly porridge, bread and vegetables, with a little meat or fish occasionally. They became dissatisfied with these harsh conditions and three rebellions happened in the 14th century.

The first revolt was in Flanders (now in Belgium). It began in 1323 and lasted until 1328. The peasants and farmers refused to pay their taxes. The landlords resisted them, and civil war erupted. A French army finally crushed it.

In northern France, the second revolt was a protest against hordes of mercenary soldiers ravaging the

1 **Norfolk**
2 **Huntingdon**
3 **Cambridge**
4 **Suffolk**
5 **Hertford**
6 **Essex**
7 **Middlesex**
8 **Surrey**
9 **Kent**

▲ *The counties shown are the main areas involved in the English Peasants' Revolt of 1381. The towns marked were also areas of discontent.*

▼ *As the Lord Mayor of London killed Wat Tyler on the left, the young Richard II faced the angry mob of peasants and shouted, 'I will be your leader'.*

JOHN BALL

A priest and a leading agitator of his day, John Ball was in jail in Maidstone, Kent when the Peasants' Revolt began. The rebels broke open the prison and freed him, planning to make him archbishop of Canterbury. At Blackheath he preached to the rebels, 'When Adam dalf (dug) and Eve span, wo was thanne the gentilman?' After the revolt Ball was tried and hanged.

▲ *A typical scene taken from the Duke of Berry's book* The Very Rich Hours. *It shows peasants still bound by society into working for the lord of the manor.*

countryside in 1358. Known as the *Jacquerie* because the term of contempt for a peasant was Jacques Bonhomme or 'Goodman Jack', the rebellion was savagely put down. Some 20,000 French peasants were killed.

The third revolt was in England. In 1381 people had to pay a new tax, called Poll Tax, of one shilling. That was a week's wages for a skilled labourer and peasants protested in Essex, Kent and six other counties. Led by Wat Tyler and the priest John Ball, 60,000 Kentish and Essex men marched on London, demanding to see King Richard II.

The 14-year-old Richard met the rebels on Blackheath (now in south-east London), and agreed to an end to serfdom and better labour conditions. Tyler was killed by the Lord Mayor of London, William Walworth, but Richard prevented an ugly scene by promising to be the rebels' champion. They went away satisfied, but parliament did not honour any of Richard's promises.

1380 France: Charles VI becomes king (to 1422). England: John Wycliffe and others translate the Bible into English.
1381 England: Peasants march on London burning and killing in the Peasants' Revolt. Richard II promises reforms.
1382 England: John Wyclif is expelled from Oxford University because he opposes Church doctrines. Scotland: The Scots, with a French army, attack England. Portugal: John I is king (to 1433), founder of the Avis dynasty.
1383 Tamerlane conquers Persia.
1386 Switzerland: The Swiss defeat and kill Leopold III of Austria. Spain: John of Gaunt leads an expedition to Castile (fails 1388).
1388 Mongolia: Chinese forces drive the Mongols out of their capital, Karakorum.

A plough of the 12th century was pulled by oxen to increase the amount of work that could be done. The design remained almost unchanged until the 16th century.

1389 England: Richard II, aged 22, assumes power. Scotland: A truce halts fighting between England and the French and Scots. Great Schism: Boniface IX becomes pope at Rome (to 1404).
1390 Scotland: Robert III, king (to 1406). Ottoman empire: Turks complete conquest of Anatolia.
1391 First siege of Constantinople by Turks (to 1398): Constantinople pays Turks tribute (money). Russia: Tamerlane defeats Toqtamish, khan of the Golden Horde.
1392 France: Charles VI goes mad. Korea: Yi Song-gye seizes power and founds the Yi dynasty (to 1910).

Society and Government

There were many different types of government at this time. In China, the emperor had complete power over a vast area of land. In contrast, towns in Italy such as Venice made their own rules separately.

In theory, England was ruled by a king and his council, but in reality the king had all the power. In Europe, the feudal society still kept people firmly in their places for most of this period, but a class of wealthy merchants was gradually developing.

Throughout the world, religious leaders also had a lot of power. The Aztecs and Incas were ruled by priests, as well as by emperors. The Arabs were ruled by Islamic Law and in Europe the pope and his envoys were more powerful than many kings and emperors. The balance of power between religious leaders and kings and emperors frequently led to conflict.

▲ Edward I of England in Parliament in 1274. The Church taught that kings were appointed by God and that it was everyone's duty to obey them. But a weak king could find himself overthrown.

▶ The Incas celebrated two festivals of the Sun. One was in June, the other in December. The emperor led the ceremonies in the great square at Cuzco. Officials from all over the empire attended.

▶ In the Islamic empire, the Koran gave women important rights over property. For example, when a woman married, her bridegroom had to give her a dowry. This became her own property, even if she was later divorced.

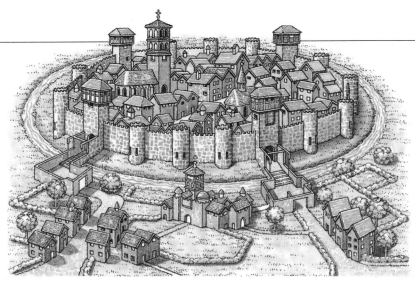

WHEN IT HAPPENED

1192 Minamoto Yoritomo becomes shogun of Japan and takes over real power.

1215 In England the Magna Carta gives rights to the barons.

14th century Peasants revolt in much of Europe demanding better pay and conditions.

▲ Most medieval towns were built in the same pattern. This example is Feurs, in the south of France. The walls protected the town from attack and also helped to control trade – tolls could be collected from strangers carrying goods.

▲ Rich men carried their money in purses on their belts to prevent robbery. Rich and poor people could usually be told apart by their clothes.

1393 Tamerlane takes Baghdad and subdues Mesopotamia (present-day Iraq).

1394 Ireland: Richard II of England leads expedition to conquer Ireland. The Great Schism: Benedict XIII antipope at Avignon (to 1423).

1396 England: Richard II marries seven-year-old Princess Isabelle of France. Anatolia: Abortive crusade by about 20,000 European knights against Turks is defeated at Nicopolis. Ottoman empire: Turks conquer Bulgaria.

A Turkish door knocker in the shape of two winged dragons. Dragons had an astrological significance and were thought to protect the buildings on which they hung.

1397 Scandinavia: Union of Kalmar unites Norway, Denmark and Sweden under Eric of Denmark. Ottoman empire: Turks invade Greece.

1398 India: Tamerlane ravages kingdom of Delhi and massacres 100,000 prisoners.

1399 England: John of Gaunt dies and his eldest son, Henry of Bolingbroke, is banished by Richard II. Bolingbroke invades England, deposes Richard and becomes Henry IV (to 1413).

1400 England: Richard II is murdered at Pontefract Castle. Wales: Owen Glendower proclaims himself prince of Wales and begins rebellion.

15th century By this date Indonesian traders regularly visit Australia's north coast to collect sea-slugs and sandalwood. These goods are traded as far away as China.

1402 Wales: Henry IV of England enters Wales in pursuit of Glendower. Ottoman empire: Tamerlane overruns most of it, which saves the Byzantine empire.

1403 England: Henry IV defeats and kills Harry 'Hotspur' Percy at the battle of Shrewsbury after the Percy family rebel.

The Fall of Constantinople

In eastern Europe and the Near East two empires vied for power in the late Middle Ages. One was the remains of the Christian Byzantine empire (capital Constantinople). The other was the Muslim Ottoman empire, founded in about 1299 by the Turk Osman I.

The Ottoman Turks built up their empire quickly. From 1326 they proceeded to conquer large parts of the Byzantine empire. They controlled most of Greece, Bosnia, Albania and Bulgaria by 1450, and tried to conquer Hungary. All that was left of the Byzantine empire was Constantinople, which was founded on a village once called Byzantium.

In 1453 the Turks, under Mehmet II (Muhammad II), made a final assault on the city. The last Byzantine emperor, Constantine XI, had about 10,000 men under arms whereas Mehmet had between 100,000 and 150,000 soldiers. Mehmet could not send his warships

◀ *A janissary, an elite soldier of the Ottoman army. The name came from the Turkish word for 'new forces', because the first janissaries were prisoners of war.*

into the Golden Horn, a channel of sea which runs through Constantinople, because it was guarded by a huge iron chain. So he dragged 70 small ships overland to launch an attack. Protected by strong walls, the Byzantine forces held out for 54 days before Mehmet's best troops, the *janissaries*, overran the city. This was the end of the Byzantine empire.

▲ *After Constantinople fell the Turks converted the Christian church of St Sophia into a mosque.*

▲ *Turkish decorative arts were very distinctive. This panel dates from the Seljuk period.*

▼ *Teams of oxen and thousands of soldiers dragged the 70 small galleys (oared warships) of Mehmet II's fleet along a wooden track over a neck of land into the unprotected part of the Golden Horn.*

1403 Tamerlane withdraws from Anatolia. China: Yung Lo is emperor (to 1424). A 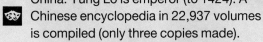 Chinese encyclopedia in 22,937 volumes is compiled (only three copies made).

1404 The Great Schism: Innocent VII, pope at Rome (to 1406). Persia: Shah Rukh (fourth son of Tamerlane) rules (to 1447).

1405 Wales: French soldiers land to support Glendower against the English. Mongolia: Tamerlane dies on his way to campaign in China; his empire disintegrates. Ottoman empire: Civil war starts (to 1413). China: Zheng He embarks on his first expedition.

The standard of the French heroine and war leader, Joan of Arc.

1406 The Great Schism: Gregory XII is pope at Rome (to 1415). Scotland: James I, aged 12, is king (to 1437); the English seize him on his way to France and hold him captive (to 1423). Wales: Henry, Prince of Wales, defeats Glendower.

1409 The Council of Pisa is called to resolve the Great Schism; it declares the rival popes deposed and elects a third, Alexander V (to 1410).

1410 John XXIII (Baldassare Cossa), is antipope at Pisa (to 1415). Holy Roman Empire: Sigismund is emperor (to 1437).

1411 India: Ahmad Shah, ruler (to 1422), builds the beautiful city Ahmadabad as his capital in western India.

1413 England: Henry V is king (to 1422). Ottoman empire: Mehmet I consolidates Ottoman power (to 1421).

1414 Italy: The Medici family of Florence become bankers to the papacy.

1415 Hundred Years War: Henry V of England revives claim to the French throne and defeats French at Agincourt. North Africa: Prince Henry the Navigator of Portugal captures Ceuta.

End of Hundred Years War

After a long truce the Hundred Years War started up again in 1415. Henry V, England's adventurous king, revived his country's old claim to the throne of France. England still held Calais and parts of Bordeaux.

Henry captured the town of Harfleur in Normandy, and also heavily defeated the French at Agincourt losing only about 1600 men to France's 10,000. He next occupied much of northern France and forced the French king, Charles VI, to disinherit his own son and make Henry heir to the French throne. He also married Charles's daughter, Catherine of Valois. However, Henry died only 15 months later, leaving his infant son Henry VI. Charles VI died soon after.

In support of the claim Henry's uncle, John, Duke of Bedford, besieged Orleans. French forces led by a 17-year-old peasant girl, Joan of Arc, successfully defended the town. Joan saw visions and heard voices telling her to free France. Joan escorted the new uncrowned

MAIN BATTLE DATES

1340 Sluys (E)*
1346 Crécy (E)
1347 Calais (E)
1356 Poitiers (E)
1370 Pontvallain (F)
1372 La Rochelle (F)*
1415 Agincourt (E)
1428 Orleans (F)
1429 Patay (F)
1448 Le Mans (F)
1450 Formigny (F)
1451 Bordeaux (F)

E = English victory
F = French victory
* = Naval battle

JOAN OF ARC

At 17 Joan of Arc (1412–1431) led the French against the English. At her trial she was accused of being a witch and found guilty. The verdict was later changed. In 1920 she was made a saint.

▲ A stained-glass window shows Joan of Arc, France's heroine.

French king, Charles VII, to Reims to be crowned. But shortly afterwards she was defeated at Paris and captured by the Burgundians. They sold her to the English who burned her as a witch.

Sporadic fighting carried on for some years. The French recaptured their lands, effectively ending the war and leaving only Calais to the English.

▲ Joan of Arc kneeling before the King of France. She said she was guided by the voices of saints Michael, Catherine and Margaret. She is shown in the armour she wore from the start of her campaign to her death.

▼ At the battle of Agincourt, Henry V commanded only about 900 men-at-arms and 3000 archers. The French had at least three times as many heavily armed troops, but they were badly led and organized.

Henry the Navigator

Prince Henry the Navigator was not a navigator (a sailor who plotted a ship's direction) and never attempted to explore, but he was called the Navigator because through his encouragement Portuguese sailors began to explore the coast of Africa.

Henry was the third son of King John I of Portugal. At the age of 21 he led a Portuguese army to capture the Moorish city of Ceuta in North Africa. There he found treasures that had been brought across the desert from the Senegal River in West Africa. He wondered if this river could be reached by sea.

The date of his first expediton is not known, but between 1424 and 1434, Henry sent 14 expeditions along the west coast of Africa. None of them would sail beyond the dangerous seas off Cape Bojador, on the coast of the western Sahara. But the 15th expedition did.

Encouraged by this, Henry built a school of navigation at Sagres on the southern coast of Portugal. From his home there he sent more expeditions to

▲ The Portuguese developed what was then the perfect ship for exploration, the caravel. It was small, with a crew of only 30 men. Its triangular or lateen sails enabled it to sail very close to the wind.

◄ At Sagres, Henry established a school which brought together the best navigators and geographers of Europe. They helped to plan and equip his expeditions, and to train the crews. His captains and pilots were taught navigation, astronomy and cartography (map making). New designs were produced for the expeditions' ships. Henry also had an observatory built to help ships navigate by the stars.

PRINCE HENRY

Henry (1394–1460) captured Ceuta in 1415. He was made governor of the Algarve in 1419 and lived at Sagres. In 1443 he was given a monopoly of African exploration.

THE PHOENICIANS

The Portuguese were not the first sailors to try to sail round the coast of Africa. The Phoenicians (*see* pages 56–57), under contract to the ruler of Egypt, sailed round Africa in about 600 BC. Their ships were driven by oarsmen and it must have taken over two years for them to complete the voyage. On their return, however, the Egyptian ruler did not make use of their discoveries.

explore the west coast of Africa. Gradually his sailors overcame their fear of falling off the edge of what they believed was a flat Earth. By the time Prince Henry died in 1460, Portuguese explorers had reached the coast of what is now Sierra Leone. Henry's work inspired later Portuguese explorers to sail round the Cape of Good Hope and find a sea route to India and the Far East.

ANCIENT BELIEFS

Sailing in the Middle Ages was an unknown and frightening experience. Apart from believing the Earth was flat many sailors were terrified of what they might meet in unknown waters. They told each other colourful stories of fabulous monsters, some capable of crushing a ship, which they believed lurked in the deep Atlantic Ocean.

1416 Wales: Owen Glendower dies.

1417 The Great Schism ends when the Council of Constance elects Martin V as the only rightful pope.

c. 1418 Portugal: Prince Henry the Navigator organizes the first of many expeditions to West Africa. The Portuguese discover the islands of Madeira.

1420 Hundred Years War: Henry V of England is acknowledged as heir to the French throne.

1421 Ottoman empire: Sultan Murad II becomes emperor (to 1451). China: the capital is moved to Beijing.

1422 Hundred Years War: Henry V of England and Charles VI of France die. They are succeeded by Henry VI, a baby, as King of England (to 1461) and Charles VII as King of France (to 1461).

This early 15th century bowl from Valencia, Spain, shows a Portuguese sailing ship.

1424 Hundred Years War: John, Duke of Bedford, defeats the French at Cravant. Portuguese sailors start the attempt to sail round Cape Bojador, West Africa.

1428 English begin the siege of Orleans. Joan of Arc sees visions and hears voices telling her to free France.

1429 Joan of Arc is appointed military commander and wins the siege of Orleans. Charles VII is eventually crowned king of France at Reims.

1430 Burgundians capture Joan of Arc and hand her over to the English.

Trade

The Middle Ages saw a great revival in trade within Europe. Towns and markets sprang up and many large cities held trade fairs. Merchants established contacts with the Near East again and so luxury goods such as silks and spices came into Europe once more.

Within Europe the most important trade was in wool. At first England supplied the fleeces for the cloth makers of the Low Countries to spin and weave. Later the situation changed and most of the cloth was then made in England. Banking started at this time, as did the slave trade. Merchants grew rich through buying and selling, but they also risked losing their money when they sent goods overseas. Ships might be wrecked or attacked by pirates and the cargo lost.

▲ Merchants sold local produce in the market towns of Europe. At the larger fairs merchants sold silk, brocade and porcelain from China, spices from South-East Asia, gold from Africa and jewels from India.

▼ Although going by sea was the easiest and safest way of moving goods, shipwrecks did happen. To avoid losing all their money in a shipwreck, merchants had shares in several ships. Each ship was shared between several merchants.

▲ The seal of Danzig. Danzig, on the Baltic, was one of the leading towns in the Hanseatic League which dominated the trade of northern Europe.

▶ *The first modern European bank was set up by merchants in Venice in 1171. Its purpose was to lend money to the government. Soon merchants realized that banks were useful places to deposit their money and to invest it safely. The success of the bank in Venice led to the formation of banks in all the major cities of Europe. People began to realize that banks helped to develop trade and commerce, as well as making a profit for their owners. Venice went on to establish a series of trading ports around the Mediterranean and by 1400 it had become the richest commercial city in Europe.*

WHEN IT HAPPENED

1241 Hanseatic League begins when two ports agree to protect each other's merchants.

***c.* 1290** Guilds are established in Europe.

1400 By this date there are over 150 ports in the Hanseatic League.

▲ *The use of paper money began in China in the 7th century AD. Marco Polo wrote about it in the 13th century. This note from the 14th century is made of bark paper.*

◀ *A slave market in the Yemen in 1237. The Koran did not ban slavery, but forbade people from making other Muslims into slaves. Slaves were mostly bought from central Asia and Africa.*

1431 Joan of Arc burned as a witch at Rouen. Henry VI of England is crowned king of France in Paris. Cambodia: Khmer city of Angkor is abandoned; the Thais and Chams, supported by the Mongols, rebel against their Khmer overlords and overrun most of the empire.

1432–1434 Portuguese explorers discover the islands of the Azores.

1433 West Africa: Tuaregs from the Sahara sack Timbuktu.

1434 Portuguese sailors successfully round Cape Bojador, West Africa, and go on to explore the west coast of Africa.

1436 Hundred Years War: English troops withdraw from Paris.

Heavenly dancers carved on a temple at Angkor in about 1200.

1437 Scotland: James I is murdered at Perth. James II becomes king (to 1460).

1438 France: Pragmatic Sanction of Bourges declares the French Church independent of the papacy. Holy Roman Empire: Albert II is made emperor (to 1439). Peru: Pachacuti becomes Sapa Inca and expands the Inca empire further.

1439 Papacy: Felix V becomes last of the antipopes (to 1449).

1440 Holy Roman Empire: Frederick III, emperor (to 1493); in Mainz goldsmith Johannes Gutenberg begins printing with movable type. Benin: Ewuare the Great takes the title of *oba* (king) (to 1481); he institutes many reforms and his powerful army conquers the Yoruba to the west and Lower Niger to the east.

The Khmer Empire

The Khmer empire (now Cambodia) was created in 802 when the Khmer people were united by King Jayavarman I. The Khmers wrote books on paper, palm leaves and vellum. Fire, rot and termites have long since destroyed them, but we can learn a lot about the Khmers in ancient Chinese histories, and from the carvings in the ruins of Angkor Thom, which means 'great city', and Angkor Wat, the city's 'great temple'.

Angkor Thom, originally called Yasodharapura, was begun just before 900. Angkor Wat was built between 1113 and 1150. The Khmer empire reached its height during the reign of Jayavarman VII (1181-1220).

The Khmer were builders, fishermen, farmers and warriors. Many lived in houses perched on stilts around the lake of Tonle Sap, as today's Cambodians still do. Their main food was rice and they developed an irrigation system which produced three crops a year.

The kings were Hindus, but most of the people were Buddhists. They held religious feasts to celebrate the start of

▼ *The Khmer empire was at its greatest extent during the reign of King Jayavarman VII (1181–1220).*

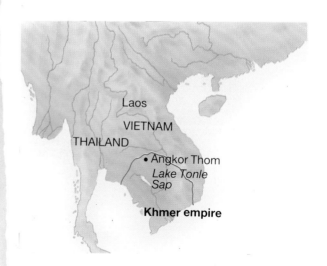

ploughing and harvest. They traded with China, bartering spices and rhinoceros horn for porcelain and lacquerware.

Sculptures show that the royal women of the court wore skirts, but left the upper part of the body bare. They were encouraged to study law, astrology and languages. Most men only wore a loose covering round their loins.

The Khmer armies, which may have included hundreds of war elephants, fought many battles and conquered most of the surrounding lands. But in the 15th century, invading armies from Thailand forced the Khmer to abandon Angkor.

▲ *Many of the temple carvings at Angkor Wat show the daily lives of the Khmer people as well as telling the stories of their sacred myths and bloody battles.*

▼ *A reconstruction of Angkor Wat. The huge, elaborate temple complex is surrounded by walls and a moat that was 180 metres wide and 4 kilometres long. The temple was made up of three main enclosures (representing the outer world) surrounding an inner holy shrine. After the temple and the city were abandoned in the 15th century, they were swallowed up by the jungle and not rediscovered until the 1860s.*

1451 Hundred Years War: French take Bordeaux and Bayeux from the English. Scotland: Glasgow University is founded. Ottoman empire: Mehmet II becomes sultan of Turkey (to 1481).

1452 Hundred Years War: English recapture Bordeaux from the French. Italy: Leonardo da Vinci, artist, architect and engineer is born (dies 1519).

1453 England, driven out of France, retains only Calais. The Hundred Years War ends. Byzantine empire: Constantinople falls to the Ottoman Turks after a siege of 54 days; it marks the end of the Byzantine empire. England: Henry VI declared insane; Richard of York is declared Protector and rules in his place.

Johannes Gutenberg who introduced printing to Europe and made it possible to produce the books we know today.

1455 Henry VI recovers. Richard of York is replaced by the Duke of Somerset, a Lancastrian. The Wars of the Roses start. Yorkists defeat Lancastrians at the first battle of St Albans.

1456 Germany: Johannes Gutenberg publishes the Bible in Latin, the first to be printed with movable type.

1458 Pius II becomes pope (to 1464).

1459 Ottoman empire: Turks conquer Serbia.

1460 England: Richard of York is defeated and killed at battle of Wakefield; Earl of Warwick captures London for the Yorkists; Yorkists capture Henry VI at battle of Northampton. Scotland: James II killed in battle against the English, is succeeded by eight-year-old son James III (to 1488). Mexico: the end of the great age of Mayan civilization. West Africa: The Portuguese explore the coast as far as Sierra Leone.

Printing in Europe

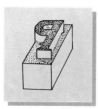

One of the most exciting developments in the Middle Ages was the European development of printing. Before then books had to be slowly and laboriously copied by hand, and only a few rich people could afford to own them. Suddenly, knowledge was within the reach of anyone who could read.

Printing was developed around 1440 by Johannes Gutenberg, a goldsmith from Mainz in Germany. His invention consisted of three parts: a mould for casting the letters in an alloy of lead, a 'sticky' ink, and a wine-press that had been adapted to make a printing press. Paper had been brought to Europe from Morocco in the 12th century.

This new method had an advantage over woodblock printing, already used for printing playing cards. Block printing needed a new block for every job, but Gutenberg's metal letters or type could be used over and over again.

▼ *The spread of printing in Europe during the first fifty years of its existence. England's first printer was William Caxton, a retired businessman.*

Gutenberg was the first of many printers who began producing books in the 15th century. They tried to match the beautiful handwritten manuscripts that had been made by the monasteries, mostly in Gothic or black-letter script. So in the first printed books Gothic type was used. Roman type, which is used in this book, was invented by Italian printers.

By 1500 there were 1700 printing presses in Europe. They had already produced around 40,000 books which were made up of nearly 20 million volumes. The invention of printing made possible the sudden spread of learning which was later called the Renaissance.

▲ *The early books were made to look as much like the familiar handwritten manuscripts as possible. Colour was added by hand after the initial printing.*

EASTERN ORIGINS

Chinese and Korean printers experimented with movable type before Gutenberg, using wood, pottery and bronze. None of their attempts was satisfactory because they faced one enormous difficulty: Chinese writing uses a minimum of 5000 different characters, and the full range is ten times as many. Even allowing for capital and small letters, numerals, punctuation marks and so on, Gutenberg needed only 300 different letters to print his first book in 1456, an edition of the Bible.

▼ *Block printing (top) required a carver to cut the letters in reverse in one solid piece of wood, which could be used for only one job. Gutenberg's metal type (bottom) could be broken up and reused.*

▶ *Early printing was carried out by rubbing a sheet of paper on to an inked woodblock. Gutenberg adapted a wine press to apply pressure quickly and evenly over the whole sheet of paper. This kind of press remained in use for the next 350 years. The ink was spread on a metal plate and then dabbed on the type with a leather-covered tool. Later on, a roller was used to apply the ink more evenly.*

War and Weapons

As the struggle for power continued, there were wars in many parts of the world. In Europe, the most important soldiers were the knights. In Japan they were the samurai. Both had very strict codes of chivalry and relied on warhorses to carry them into battle.

European knights wore heavy chain mail and metal helmets. Gradually, this was replaced by armour made from flat metal plates, which made the knight extremely heavy. An elaborate suit of armour could weigh over 45 kilos. They also began to use longer swords which were sharpened to get through plate armour.

In the 12th century, much fighting took place around castles, rather than on battlefields. Despite the development of heavily fortified castles, the technique of seige warfare differed little from that used in ancient times. By the middle of the 14th century the use of gunpowder had spread to Europe from China. Once cannons were able to knock down castle walls, the castle could no longer protect its inhabitants.

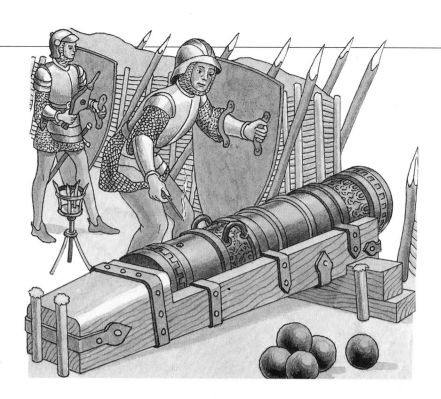

▲ *A cannon from the 14th century. It is made of strips of iron, held together with hoops. The arrival of gunpowder from China in the 13th century completely changed warfare and weapons. The first guns appeared in the 14th century and were very like simple cannons mounted on long, wooden shafts. By the middle of the 15th century the matchlock had been invented, but it was unsafe to load.*

▼ *A Japanese samurai warrior on horseback was a frightening sight. Samurai armour was made of enamelled metal links or very thick strips of leather, which made it flexible. They fought with bows and arrows and with long curved swords. A samurai's sword was his most treasured possession. It had a razor sharp edge for cutting but a soft iron core enabling it to withstand many blows.*

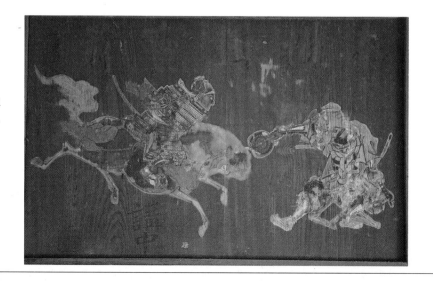

13th century The English develop the longbow.

1291 Christian Crusaders are finally thrown out of the Holy Land (Palestine).

1304 Arabs start using the first guns.

1337–1453 The Hundred Years War is fought between France and England.

1453 Constantinople falls to the Ottoman Turks after a 54-day siege.

▶ *The art of heraldry grew out of the need for knights to recognize each other on the battlefield, so that they did not kill people on their own side. To make this easier, they painted their shields with simple patterns. Soon all the men in the same army used the same pattern.*

▼ *During a seige, catapults hurled stones and giant, soldier-laden seige towers were wheeled up to the walls. Archers kept up a hail of arrows to keep defenders back.*

The Wars of the Roses

The Wars of the Roses is the name given to the struggle between two branches of the Plantagenet family (*see* pages 12–13) for the English throne. Called the House of York and the House of Lancaster, both were descended from Edward III.

Trouble began in 1453 when King Henry VI, of the House of Lancaster, went mad. His distant cousin, Richard, Duke of York, became Lord Protector (regent) and ruled for him. When Henry suddenly recovered, war broke out between Richard of York and his supporters and the Lancastrian advisers to Henry VI. Although Richard was killed, the Yorkists triumphed and in 1461 Richard's son became Edward IV. Henry VI was later murdered.

When Edward died 12 years later, his young son Edward V succeeded him, under the care of his uncle, Richard, Duke of Gloucester. After a few weeks Richard seized the throne, saying that Edward V was illegitimate. Edward and his younger brother were possibly murdered. The remaining Lancastrian heir, Henry Tudor, defeated and killed Richard, becoming King Henry VII. He married Edward IV's daughter, Elizabeth of York, and ended the Wars of the Roses.

THE ROSES

The Wars of the Roses get their name from the emblems of the two principal families involved: the red rose of Lancaster and the white rose of York.

When Henry VII became king and married Elizabeth of York he combined the two to form the Tudor Rose which is shown here.

RICHARD III	**HENRY VII**
1452 Born. Brother of Edward IV. **1471** Murder of Henry VI. Richard possibly present. **1483** Becomes Lord Protector for his nephew, Edward V; takes the throne. **1485** Dies at the battle of Bosworth Field.	**1457** Born; his mother a great granddaughter of John of Gaunt. **1471** Flees to Brittany. **1485** Defeats Richard III, becomes king. **1486** Marries Elizabeth of York, Edward IV's daughter. **1509** Dies at Richmond.

▼ Henry Tudor's army defeated and killed Richard III at the battle of Bosworth Field in Leicestershire. William Shakespeare later wrote that Richard III cried, 'A horse, a horse, my kingdom for a horse' when he was thrown on the battlefield.

Index

This index has been designed to help you find easily the information you are looking for. Page numbers in *italic* type (slanting) refer to pages on which there are illustrations.